# Amerigo Vespucci

## Barry Swan

Valley Press

First published in 1998
by Valley Press
236 Tokyngton Ave, Wembley,
Middlesex HA9 6HJ

© 1998 Barry Swan

Typeset in Meridien by LaserScript Ltd,
Mitcham, Surrey
Cover design by Linda Blakemore
Printed and bound in Ireland by Colour Books Ltd, Dublin

ISBN 0 9530768 1 4

For Chris and Natasha

# Contents

# Chapter One

It came through with some static, such as one picks up on an old, short-wave wireless.

"Hello there. Is there an Irishman in the house? Anybody from old Ireland?" When I heard these words, coming as they were from afar and in a strange, other-world tone, I could not help but shiver with a slight uncontrollable fit of excitement and, when that had passed, breathe a sigh of pleasure. For I too was from Ireland. I was as Irish as green shamrock or the Lakes of Killarney. Myself, my mother and my father and their mothers and fathers for as far back as you can go were all natives of that land, the deep, rich soil of good old Ireland. But I am not here to relate to you the details of my own tale. It pales into insignificance; it vanishes completely out of sight when one compares it with the story told to all of us in the late hours in that house one star-lit night. It is the story of a man who knew Amerigo Vespucci.

When the voice asked that most unexpected question everybody at the table immediately looked at me. A few moments passed before I realised I would have to say something. I was still taken aback by the surprise of meeting a fellow-countryman so far from home and in so strange a circumstance. The expectant faces of those sitting about me made me suddenly appreciate the importance of my predicament. As the only Irishman in the place it would be incumbent on me to talk to and explain and elaborate on whatever our welcome visitor would have to say. In fact, I was to be a mediator between a nether world and the company there present. Well, I would play my part certainly. I have always done so, whenever a crisis or problem has necessitated my particular abilities or bene-volent nature being put to use. I was doubly aware of my responsibility when I realised that the credibility of these sessions organised by me, as well as the honour of a holy country, were at stake. I would keep the backchat down to a minimum and hope that the good humour of the listening people would tide them over any incomprehen-sible "bantering" between the two of us.

"Hello there. Are ye from Ireland now?" It was me talking.

Everybody was hushed and looking at me. I knew how much the whole thing depended on me. Then the voice replied.

"You don't know how relieved I am to be able to speak to a fellow countryman." It was from very far away. One could just tell by the sound of it. Although it was strong and very much present and coherent, it seemed to wane ever so slightly after so many words, as if it was coming from millions of light years and innumerable aeons of time away. There was no doubting the accent, though what county or part of the country it was from I was not as yet sure. It seemed to have a certain modulated quality, enriched as it were by some new ingredient picked up in travel or in some unusual experience or experiences.

Anyway, as our friend from far away had quite a good yarn to tell, let us take up his story straight away without further ado. You can be assured that it was a good one, for he kept all of us there at our seats even while the glinting stars were waning and the awakening day announcing its presence.

"I knew Amerigo Vespucci." We all looked at each other. I played my part and said:

"Tell us about him." These were the last words I was to say for a long period of time.

"I'll begin at the beginning so sit back and relax. As you all probably know by now I'm from Ireland. I was not born in county Cork. In the year of fourteen hundred and forty nine I was born in Kerry where every man is fair. I don't know if you can picture what life was like in those days. Looking at the world now, I can see a lot of improvements that have taken place. All the same, I'm not sure whether I'd prefer to be living now instead of when I did. It's very hard to say. Anyway, to get back to what I was talking about, in those days there were very few people who were not dependent on the cattle. The more bulls and cows you had, the bigger the man you were. Should you by any chance have a big herd, well, you were on top of the world. And there was precious little you could get or do without a fair portion of the beasts. The cattle were different then to what they are now. They weren't as big or as fleshy then, but couldn't they give milk! Bucketfulls of it, night and morning. And they were all, each and every one, as black as soot, without exception. Black gold they were and we treated them as they deserved to be treated, like kings and queens. I myself had seven of the bastes and right beauts they were. Two bulls, two cows and three calves each of three weeks, three months and six months old. A fine prospect for the future, without a doubt. I had established my little herd years earlier when my father, Sean Mor Beag, passed out. The way we did things then was that all his cattle were divided between the seven of us, his seven sons. So, by the order of things, what was a big herd became a number of small herds overnight. The back, left-hand comer of his land became my own little domain and it was there I settled down to an innocent existence.

In my forty third year I wanted to take a wife. To tell you the honest truth, I never really wanted to be stuck with a wench. I was doing all right without one. All the same, people were talking and seldom a week passed but I had some busybody who would give me a lecture on the advantages of having one of them around the house. Anyway, to cut a long story short, there was this Pegeen MacCarthaig who lived not too far away who was suitable. She had red, fiery eyes that made me think of cow's milk whenever I looked at them. Since the lass was of the Ceann Subh MacCarthaig, I being Lamh Fada MacCarthaig and therefore of a separate branch, we got the go-ahead of sundry authorities and decided to take the plunge.

Now let me tell you what happened next. You won't believe it. One morning before the crack of dawn when it was still dark I set off for the fair of Raspuc many miles away. It was solely for the purpose of looking with pleasure at the display of animals and to speak their praises that I went. I would have to wait until my own young fellows came of age before they'd be ready for sale and I'd have some silver in my pocket to put to use. It was the thought of these pleasant days to come, as well as a meditation every now and then on my forthcoming marriage which I did not consider so pleasant, that occupied my mind on the journey to and long, roundabout journey back from the fair. One reason it took me so long to get back was that along the way was the home of a person of my acquaintance whom I had met at our own local fair and we agreed to visit one another whenever the opportunity arose. This was the first time I had ever gone to his house and it took me ages to find it as somehow the directions he gave me were not adequate. Anyway that is neither here or there. The real matter is that by the time the talk and sup was over and the road had been set upon again more time had passed than had been desired. I was two days late in going back and this was to prove my undoing for if my home place had been reached earlier, surely they would have been caught red-handed in the act?

On arrival in the vicinity of the Lamh Fada MacCarthaig baile, the morning smoke arising from the comfortable, humble shacks set together along the rumbling brook made a happy sight. The barking of a hound and the mooing of the homely cows put one's mind at peace. The mild washing of drizzle on my face cleaned my heart. Walking through the field in the direction of my own dwelling, the animals were a pleasing spectacle as they paused in their munching to look up and gaze at me as I went through. Gratitude and well-being seemed to arise out of their round eyes. They were all very content by the looks of things. Before I would enter into my house, I determined to make a scrutiny of my own stock. Not that I expected anything to be amiss; the cows had suck-calves and the herdeen (or mini-herd, to borrow a modern-day word), were in a field of plenty with the added security of the Baile near-at-hand. Who would dare attempt to fiddle with cattle when the possibility of swift and savage retribution lay close by? It was with the expectation of seeing satisfied bastes, not a little bit improved even, that I sought them out to discover that they were not there at all. I will leave your own imagination to wonder at what my heart did then. Needless to say, it behaved not in the usual manner at all. It became erratic in its beating. When after some fruitless looking it was plain to see that I had been done, words escaped my lips. Even still I am hoping that nobody heard them. The shock to my system was detrimental.

At the same time as I was scanning the horizon for a sight of the lost cattle, the image and name of the suspected thief was running through my mind. It is a further difference between your time and mine that long ago you did not have to prove a man innocent before you found him guilty. As a further illustration of the traditional and wise mentality we had then it would be true for me to admit that even as I first saw that my cows were not where they should have been, in that instant I also saw in my mind's eye what punishment I was dealing out to the guilty one. It was a punishment un-restricted and unrestrained in its severity and good effect. There is no doubt at all in my mind and heart as regards the beneficial purpose behind giving out punishment. It has a cleansing and purifying effect and this is more so the case if it happens that the one giving the punishment is also the one whom the crime was committed against in the first instance.

To get back to what I did then. The loud roar of anger was in my ears and my steps had the steady inevitability of retribution in their pace as I set out for the home place of the guilty thief. I did not look either left or right until I got there. And, Fortune be praised, the luck was with me for the man I sought was out there in his field unknowing and unprotected.

That man was Michael MacCarthaig, the father of my betrothed, Pegeen. He was a silver haired rotund individual with a smooth look. A smart-alecky, snidy one; I'd always viewed him as being an interloper. That one had married into our village and instead of giving his own name to his wench of a wife he took her's; the honourable Mac-Carthaig. No one was ever sure what his original name had been, though many opinions and versions were there, of course. It is my own opinion, although I have never been able to verify it, that the fellow was a Corkman and came over into Kerry because he had been driven out by his own people, which can't be saying much for the man, or his record or standing. One factor which increased this suspicion was the way he was able to do so well when it came to business. I'm sure he had a rake of money which he never told anyone about, not even his daughter, and his house was the finest in the baile, next of course to the Chief's and the witchdoctor's. It was the only house belonging to an ordinary, common or garden subject that had oak on its cross-beams and a door furbished with the rarest skin, that of the Ulster wolfhound. I'd like to know where he got that? It was the cunning way he managed to conceal all this in his everyday talk and the way he conversed with one while at the same time pulling the wool over your eyes that gave me a stomach ache. The sneaky underhand manner in which he was improving his house and stocking his herd, in a fashion so quick as to be miraculous, and generally beginning to take on the appearance of a Texas millionaire, would be enough to give anyone the pip.

How could a man advance his fortune so effortlessly without having obvious talents of any extraordinary calibre or any other advantages over those of his neighbour, may I ask? And what is more. How could a herd of normal looking cattle increase in size three-fold over the short period of one year? Can a cow produce three calves in one year and in that same year raise them up to the prime condition of mature cattle ready for the slaughter?

Maybe they do in Cork but they don't in Kerry.

Shouting something like "you thieving son of Satan's daughter, I'll throttle you" I leapt on him and in less than a minute, betime you could say "Jack Robinson", he was stone dead. Wringing his neck was a very enjoyable matter and could you blame me? A twister like him? The next moment even as I was on top of the thief, there came from behind me an almighty screech and bellowing and the sound of running feet. Before I could turn around I felt my hair being ripped from off my head and claws scratching my face.

Her language let me say, was choice. It was worse than I had ever used or even heard before. It was the thin screeching of a bitter wench. You may, by now, have suspected who this irate bitch happened to be. With my head bent and twisted at an acute angle because of her grip, I could just make out behind her raw arms the upside down head of the man's daughter, Pegeen, my so-called betrothed.

Heaving myself up I lashed out with a terrific wallop and caught her on the puss. She released her hold on me and fell quickly to the earth. She lay there by her dad and I thought that they just deserved each other. I'm sorry, but I have no pity at all for the likes of them and I'm not an uncharitable man. I'll give any person his due if he deserves it, but I have no time for people who filch on their neighbours. Fair is fair after all and charity and forgiveness may be all right in the text books and to teach young children in the schools and in the home, but who can deny that, with that thief lying dead there, justice had been done? Some people in the modern world today would say that I had taken "the law into my own hands" and "usurped the jurisdiction of the courts" and so on but you have got to remember that we had no policemen then, so how can you talk about law and courts and those things?

How, I ask you again, can you have courts and laws without policemen? It is like having a cart without a horse.

This was my defence when I was called before Chief MacCarthaig and his assembly of jurors, clerics, doctors and henchmen to explain myself. It impressed them and the Chief said that I had a point.

I sat back on the low wooden stool and rested my shoulders against the proximate wall, awaiting their verdict as they conversed with each other. They were at it a long time. It is a pity that there weren't the comforts in those days that there are now; like backs on chairs for instance. My rear was cramped from its uncomfortable position and aching badly as the Chief turned to address me again.

"There is just one point which puzzles us. Why is it that there's no sign or trace of your cattle on the man's land, or anywhere else as a matter of fact? If he stole them, surely it follows as clearly as night follows day that he should have them?"

You may have noticed by now that I was no amadan in those days and I soon put them right on that one.

"Don't be so naive. You are very easily taken in. If you nabbed your neighbours cattle would you leave them out in the open air for everyone to see them? If you would, then you'd be more stupid than I think you are." They looked puzzled and they stared at each other for quite a long time. Then the Chief spoke again, with great doubt and uncertainty in his deep voice.

"If they are not out in the open air, do you think it is possible that they might be hidden inside somewhere, or even underground?"

"That is the most ridiculous thing I have heard said yet. Now where in the name of the moon and stars do you think he could have put them? Inside his pocket? Or under the cabbages in his garden? If he did that, well then you may be assured that he did not steal them at all in the first place for the simple reason that that is an impossible thing to do, if only because of the awkward size that seven animals make. No. He did not put them inside anywhere or under anything. Believe me. In fact, that he did not do this is one of the things that points to his definite guilt. How could a person, so cunning, do such a stupid thing? It would be a contradiction of fact, reason and the general order of nature."

They all agreed with me, as I could see from their nodding heads and respectful looks.

"No. It is my own belief that he either drove them, with the connivance of his daughter, away over the border to Cork where I believe he had many contacts, or, maybe even more likely, he had a special squad come to do the job for him. A very cunning man he was without a doubt. I don't know how long he has been at this racket but I'd say he was no simple beginner. And who knows whose cattle would have been next? Maybe even your's Chief, if I may respectfully say so."

"That is true", he replied thoughtfully.

"I am in no doubt that I have done the community at large a service by getting rid of that one."

"Agreed", said the Chief.

Then from the Chief's side the cleric spoke. It was the first time he had spoken since the opening of the proceedings.

"There is still one thing that bothers me. What you say about there being no policeman could be true I suppose and there may be a case for you for taking the law into your own hands, in the eyes of the Chief here and of the world. But, is there justice in what you did in the eyes of God? Was your act morally justified? This is my conundrum."

Needless to say, I developed an intense dislike of that man there and then. There was great annoyance and strain in my voice as I answered him. "What is justice, may I ask? Surely it is the rewarding of the good and the punishment of the guilty?"

"That is what the holy church teaches. Correct."

"Would it be justice to reward the guilty and punish the innocent?" "No."

"Then in that case you could hardly expect me to remunerate or reward that man. Could you? To do so would be the act of a simpleton or madman. Am I not right in what I'm saying?"

"You are."

"Well then, if I couldn't reward him and at the same time justice needed to be done, surely there was no alternative left but to punish him?"

"I suppose you're correct there. In my opinion, I must follow suit with my colleagues on the bench here and declare you innocent and guiltless. But there are certain qualms and doubts that I have of my own which I'll keep to myself and let God be the final arbiter of things in the long run. It is a funny world. You are found not guilty and are free to go, as far as I am concerned."

At that the Chief made a gesture that all was finished and done with and then a beam of a smile came over his face. They left their seats together and came across to congratulate me. I was extremely delighted to be able to get up and stretch my back for it was in a terrible way. I shook their hands, one by one, with great pleasure. I was so relieved that I even found myself being friendly to the person who had asked that awkward question about justice. We conversed and chatted away there for a long time. Eventually the Chief asked my about my plans. I told him.

"I have come to the conclusion that after all that has happened and with the breakdown of my marriage plans, there is nothing to keep me here and I will go away. It has always been my ambition to travel and see the world and I'm not too old to do that yet. What with the loss of all my cattle and having nothing to my name except my forty three years there is little I can lose by going. And who knows what I might gain?"

"It is your decision and we wish you well", said the Chief.

Then, to my astonishment, he said that they had a surprise for me and would I leave the room for a moment?

I was outside for what seemed like ages. It was beginning to drizzle again and I was wishing they would hurry up. Eventually a shout called me back in and there they all were bunched together and grinning like Cheshire cats. The Chief held his hands behind his back and it was obvious he was holding something there.

"Close your eyes", said he in a jocose tone.

What follows is one of those mysteries of life that has no answer or solution in the realms of reason or logic. I have never been able to understand why they did what they did.

A heavy object was placed in my arms and when I opened my eyes I saw that it was a leather bag. It was full of something. I opened it. Inside were heaps and heaps of gold. Pure gold, nuggets and coins of the newest quality. I would say there was enough in it to make a man wealthy for life. Even by today's standards what it came to in pounds was enviable, a major fortune by any reckoning. I was assured it was mine.

"It will help you on your way and smoothen your path for you and enable you to overcome any obstacles the evil one puts in your way", said the Chief. Still not believing it, I bade them good bye and thanks and lobbing the priceless bag over my shoulder, went outside into the falling rain.

# Chapter Two

Before I could leave, I would have to say good bye and adios to all my relations. It is a common courtesy and I am sorry to see that it is dying out in certain countries; though not all, let me say. It is gratifying to find that there are at least one or two people still keeping up the old values and traditions.

To get back to the farewell festivities. I went around to every house and home which lodged a relative of mine or a friend and spent much time with each, even if some were rather distant relations and I had not seen or contacted them for ages. And in each home I was given a warm-hearted welcome and treated to much food and entertainment. It would be the early hours before I'd leave any place. In the course of time I had gone to see the MacCarthaigs of Baile More and Baile Beag; Bailenabo and Cnocbotharbailenabo; of Bailenapairce and Cnocbotharinaicebailenapairce; of Dun, Lis and Coill. They were all a lively and sporting lot.

I paid respects too to Laidir MacCarthaig, who was known to have heaved a full-sized cow single-handed across the river Le. A friendly chap who despite his great size, was as timid and as quiet as a mouse. I looked in on Siuil MacCarthaig, well known all over for his walking feats. It was said that he first discovered his ability when he went up country as a young soldier with a band on horseback. He got lost on the way back and then, to top things off, as he stepped from his mount for a split second for a recreation at the side of the road, the nag made away with a lively trot. It was left to our man to walk the two hundred miles home. This he did in the remarkable record time of one week ensuring his fame for posterity. Despite his fame and high standing, I found him a modest fellow and very easy to get on with.

Then a call was made on Eist MacCarthaig. If ever there was a strange individual in Kerry here was one. His particular claim to distinction was the unequalled sense of hearing he had. Voices and sounds of the most unusual nature and originating from the strangest of faraway places were audible to his gifted ears even while nobody else could decipher as much as a single sound or word. He was employed as the night watchman of all the herds in his own Baile, for he claimed that not the slightest irregular shuffling or commotion could ever escape his ears. He was attuned to the sighs and breathing of every baste within the radius of the village. What is more, he did this even as he lay deep asleep in his bed, asserting that then he was able to concentrate much better. A peculiar man, whom I was never able to get to know well.

Feach MacCarthaig was only a very distant relation, but he lived in the same area as Eist and since I called in on him, I decided that I might as well call in on Feach as well. Feach's eyes to look at were nothing above the ordinary.

They were just ordinary eyes of a plain grey colour and slightly dimmed with age and use if anything. But when they were put to work, the eyes of Feach MacCarthaig were anything but ordinary. They were gifted. He was reputed to be able to see into the inside of cattle and animals in general and whether this was due to a mechanical quality of the eye or simply a gift of God, was not known. It is my opinion that since to see into the interior of humans was not within his capacity, it was the latter that was responsible. Because of this talent, he was well-qualified for the diagnosing of diseases and ailments of every shade and colour that affected the cows. Employed as the medicine man for the farms around, he believed that diagnosis was as good as a cure and consequently did not believe in giving medicine or treatment of any kind. In conversation, I found him a bit obsessive about the innards of animals and medicine generally but all the same, a good-willed gent, this indispensable and trusted friend of the farmer.

I went to Bailedegort to call in on Brog Micheart (Wrong Boot) MacCarthaig who had never been able to walk in a line or direction that could ever even to the slightest degree be considered within a shade of being straight.

Many good willed efforts by friends and neighbours to teach him to walk in a straight line were to no avail. He was, to be true, the butt of many jokes and wisecracks in the district and it was said that his land was littered with numerous criss-cross tracts coming and going from the most unlikely corners and never straight, not even for two consecutive steps. Another thing that made people laugh, quite unfairly, was the fact that he made his cows go the way he always wanted to go, so that in the long run they became like himself. To my surprise, he was a very jocose person and we had a great laugh together.

By the end of the last week before I left I had also managed to put in visits to the following uncles, cousins and nephews and their families:

The MacCarthaigs Sean, Liam, Padraig, Peadair, Dermoid, Micheal, Tadgh, Christoir, Seamus, Cormac, Fionbar, Gearoid, Seosamh, Stiofan, Mairtin, Antoin, Brendain, Tomas, Eamonn, Donal, Dominic, Roibeard, Nollaig, Brian, Donncachadha; Caoimhin, Desmoind, Pol, Risteard, Oilibheir, Oilibheir Og, Mor, Beag, Risteard Og. Mor, Dubh, Pol Mor, Maol, and Pol Fada – a close first cousin and very like me in physical appearance, Desmoind Og and Beag – two right bowsies, Caoimhin an Madra, Beag and Caol, Donncachadha Mor, Ocras, Spota (Spotty), Og, Brian Ramhair (Fat), Nollaig Mor, Og, Dubh, Feargach, Cleasta, and Nollaig Tapaidh, or Noel the Hare as he was sometimes called. Roibeard Ban, Mor, Beag, Og, Dominic ganlamhamhain, Donal ganaoncluas, Og, Eamonn ganashron, Mor and Eamonn of the wide behind, Tomas an beal mor, Brendain Mall, Og, Antoin Gaireach, Mor, Dearg, Mairtin Bronach, Stiofan Og, Caol, Seosamh an lamh laidir, Gearoid Ramhair, Fionbar Cliste, Beag, Cormac Saibhreas, Seamus Bocht, Beag, Christoir ganchiall, Tadgh Mor, Tadgh Caol, Micheal Og, Beag, Mor, Dermoid an bo, Ban, Peadair Gaireach – a right clown, Padraig an cat, Og, Holy Padraig, Liam Mor and Liam Beag. There were too some female relatives who were spinsters and whom I went out of my way to see:

Maire, Brid, Peg, Pegeen (not the other Pegeen), Clair, Christin, Fiolamiona, Seosamhin and her sister, Bernadine, Patricia and Aine MacCarthaig, a woman of the most dignified and gentle disposition who was believed to be incredibly rich. Aine, who was my grandaunt, gave some encouragement to help me on my way when she assured me that there was no better or wiser thing that a young fellow of my age could do than travel to far places and if she had been even half as young again she'd be away at the drop of a hat. It helped my peace of mind somewhat that such a wise old bird should be able to see into the intelligent decision behind my going. I assured her I would write to her, no matter how far away I was, and ensure the dispatch of the letter by some efficient means. She came to the door to see me out and slipped a valuable gold bracelet into my hand before I left.

"Spare a thought for me if you get to Rome and make a petition in my name there. You will never be outside my prayers."

There were tears in my eyes as I left, for she had overseen my early years, my own mum being many years dead. I felt sorry to be leaving now, and a resolve to send that letter was set in my heart.

The blackbirds and thrushes had already started when the door of the house was pulled for the last time and the morning-pale horizon approached with firm feet and a face full of awareness and determination. Woollen under-clothes kept vulnerable flesh warm and a coat and trousers of well-beat leather was as my armour and for the present, my closest friend. Bare feet were enclosed in leather sandals with openings for the toes to protrude. Over my back were slung my only possessions in a bound up bag, attached to a long stick which was gripped in my right band.

I cannot for the life of me understand how so much nostalgia and misconstrued romanticism came to be associated with such a way of going places. How is it that whenever people dream of travelling with a free and easy heart and have all kind of interesting and exciting adventures, they are invariably carrying this ludicrous bag and stick with them? It is easy to see that they are only dreams and imaginings. It is absolutely no way to travel. If I had a horse handy just then, I would as surely have been on it as my name is Fada MacCarthaig. Oh. Did I not tell you my full name? I am called Fada, or "long".

A day of travel passed. Then the black of night prevented me from being able to see even my own hands. There is almost no wild nightlife in Ireland. At least there was none then, mainly I suppose because of the harder time it was to scrape a living and the birds and animals were just too tired to go about singing and hooting and so on at night. It was also more dangerous because certain predatory species were extant; wolves, wildcats, eagles and hawks especially, who remained purposefully silent as they prowled around. It was as quiet as it was dark as I strained my ears, turning them this way and then that way and cocking my head.

I could hear a horse coming with a fast gallop in the distance. It must have been coming in my direction for it was along by the only track way for miles. Its gallop was steady but not too rapid.

With an exactness that is learnt by necessity and need in the space of an instant, a calculated drop brought me from the bow of a big oak on to the back of a strong horse. He was mine. From the moment I felt myself alone on his speeding summit, tearing through the empty night, it was no longer the old, timid, diffident Fada MacCarthaig who was existing, but a newly created hero full of strength and ballyho. I felt like quite a different man than I had been even moments before when the mystery of the forest was getting on my nerves. Maybe it was the horse that did it and the feeling of exhilaration was purely temporary. After all I am by nature a shade despondent and subdued in character. But then it could have been an augur of a fundamental shift in the nature of my personality caused possibly by recent events. The last person to comment on a character is the character in question itself, or should be, and so I will leave it to you who are listening to make your own judgements. Suffice for me to say that I believe that there is more than one side to me.

Amerigo had a few things to say about me. I don't know whether you will agree with him or not. That comes later.

What I will do is give you a few insights into certain aspects of me. I am basically quiet, cautious and peace-loving. I prefer modesty to pomposity. I had never harmed even a mouse until that fateful day when I discovered my cattle were missing. Then I took great delight in punishing Micheal MacCarthaig. This I consider to be out of character with me and I hoped that I would not have to do anything like it ever again. A person should only indulge in such stuff if it is necessitated by defence or retribution or maybe the prevention of some misdeed. I can say with an easy conscience that I have followed these rules. Anything bad or incorrect that ever happened around me was never of my own doing; it was always due to some external cause. Events happened around me, as it were.

All the same, some change came over me when I left home. The feelings of independence and sense of adventure were new for instance. The old Fada seemed to have been left behind. New thoughts were entering my head, a different order of priority of things established themselves. A thing that started to worry me after this was the question of whether I was the same "Person" as I was before. Something told me that my head would not work and react as it used to and this was to cause me quite a lot of concern when it came to meeting important situations and problems. I did not know what my actions and reactions were to be. At that particular time of course we knew next to nothing about the ins and outs of psychology and the subconscious element in our make-up. I remember spending the first few weeks after leaving the baile screwing myself up into quite a state attempting to understand certain questions about myself. These thoughts and figurings would be going through my mind automatically as it were, as I rode along. At the very same time entirely different topics and subjects would be in my mind, common-of-fact matters like what kind of weather lay overhead or the interest of a passing baile and associated land, field, stock and accessories. There was only one element in the world which I didn't want to see and would turn the back of my head to whenever one came into view and that was, funnily enough, people.

So from what has been said it is clear that there were two strands of activities involved in the process of my actual thinking. They were two simultaneous, parallel and entirely distinct entities. Needless to say of course I was not aware of this at the time. But I was aware of something. What this thing, if that is the word, was exactly was not too plain and this strange obscurity was the cause of an amount of concern and anxiety in me. Later I concluded it had to do with the process of parallel thinking that was going on, but it is a problem that had its origin somewhere else, I think.

What was this thing, you are asking?

It had something to do with what was being said a few moments back. About me wondering whether I was the same person after I left home as I had been before. This problem has been delved into by the great scholars and philosophers of old who lived long before even my time (which goes to show you how long back they were). They studied this very question under various names and titles, one of the more common and frivolous being the denotation "change". They never solved it apparently. In Paris, later, I was to meet a very interesting chap, a runaway ex-member at the church I believe he was, who told me about the philosophers and the questions they used to discuss.

He said that despite all their hard thinking and involved discussions none of them ever succeeded in solving the important questions. In fact, he said, in his quick-witted manner, the only thing they did succeed in doing was to simply ask the very same questions all over again, only in a more clear and detailed way which had the effect of worsening the problem for whoever asked the question in the first place.

Actually, it was not chiefly the problem of who I was yesterday which was my main concern, especially since I wanted to forget all about the past and begin a new existence. What was biting me now was the query who was I at present and had the same person slipped through from the past. I doubted it. And later cognition was to confirm me in this doubt.

There was a gust in the air and I was jaunting along fairly contentedly in my own way. Then something began to happen which let me know that the crudely made affair of raw leather from cow that was my saddle was slipping. I managed to halt the horse and disembark just before I was about to fall off accidentally.

Well, bending down the fault was discovered and the process of remedying it was begun. Here is what happened next.

Didn't a horse come along at a fast gallop and pull up just behind me. I heard a voice.

"Is there anything wrong? Can I be of some help?", it asked. Now those surely were the words of well-disposed and friendly person.

Normally, I would have greeted him courteously with a wide smile and explained what the problem was. Wouldn't you?

That is not what happened in the event at all and this will show you what I mean when I say a new character had attached itself to the old. In fact, the exact order of things after that is not too clear at all. I remember saying something like:

"This nag is not to your liking my man. He has a bad saddle. You can't help me at all".

With that, I grabbed him from off his mount by the leg and had left him a sorry bleeding mess by the time I was on my way again.

You must believe me when I say I was sorry almost immediately it was done because by nature I am a peaceable man. This I have already testified to you.

How could such a tragic thing happen then?

An honest question that deserves the best answer that can be given, within the bounds of respectability.

It can be answered for by the brand new personality that had suddenly formed. It formed within and without as I removed myself into new and completely different sur-roundings. And it would be the height of nonsense and ridicule to expect a different person, a total stranger, to have the same opinions and reactions and do the same things as oneself. So you see, why what happened to that fellow took place, took place because in my opinion it was necessary and justified, due to his eyeing my horse, just as it was necessary to punish Micheal MacCarthaig, but for different reasons.

Obviously, it would take time and patience to get used to my new character and being, just as it takes time and effort to adjust to anything new. It was this process of adjustment which was causing my mind to partake in novel and diverging streams of thought and urges and after a while I came out with a very interesting and distinct character that led Amerigo Vespucci to introduce me to his friends in Spain as a man, he said, "the likes of which I have never seen or was ever seen in this realm or that of Florence or in any known land – or his speech and manner, as either displays itself''. I do not know what he went on to say for he used words abstruse in meaning and prolonged in the saying. I know that my presence and what Amerigo was telling them had a big effect on all those present because they were standing about in silence and gaping at me speechless and open-mouthed.

To get back to that tragic incident.

Much later I had a talk with the philosopher already mentioned about the whole affair. Pedro was his name.

"Pedro. Say. Just imagine. If it happened that I killed a man should I be blamed for it?"

After a little puzzled thought, he replied; "Yes."

"Say I killed a man yesterday would I be blamed for it today?" With no hesitation he replied;

"Yes, yes."

"If I killed him yesterday, should I be blamed for it yesterday?" "Si, Si," he said quickly and a little bit impatiently. Pedro was always uneasy whenever I had a serious debate with him. Later on I did not even bother to raise philosophical matters.

"And if I killed him today would I be blamed for it tomorrow?"

"Yes. Si."

"If I killed him yesterday, should I be blamed tomorrow?" "Si. Yes."

"And the day after tomorrow?"

"Si."

"And next week, and next moon and next season and next year?"

"Yes."

"And right on into the future?"

"Certainly."

"And if I killed a man today would I be blamed for it yesterday?"

"Yes."

I repeated the question slowly, deliberately and with emphasis.

"No," was his eventual reply, "you would not be blamed."

"Or if I killed him tomorrow I should not be blamed today either."

"True."

"What is troubling me is why that should be so, as it appears that the particular day a crime takes place is relevant to the particular guilt."

"I don't know," was Pedro's short answer.

I could see that Pedro was bamboozled and irritated. I felt a slight upsurge of satisfaction. Clearly he had not thought about it before and he must have felt somewhat taken aback by this revelation of a gap in his understanding. And Pedro was a straight-thinking man who was practised in the art of free-expression centuries previous to the famous free-thinkers and philosophers you read about today.

The answer of course (and Pedro came to see this himself after some persuasion from your's truly), would be that a person is not the same person at all but an entirely different individual the moment an alteration occurs either in time or space. I am a new man with each step of my foot and each tick of the clock.

What I happened to do yesterday is of no concern today. Who I was yesterday has no relevance to who I am today.

I hope you understand my line of thought now because it has a great bearing on what you are going to think of me as a responsible human being and member of the human race. Nobody likes to be misjudged or misunderstood or misinterpreted in any of his actions. You must take me as you find me right in the present and at no other time whatever. If you are going to start griping and taking moral and puritanical tones and attitudes, it would be too bad from the point of view of obtaining what intelligent, detached and unbiased observers would consider as being objective opinions. Instead you will sink into what to every other thinking person but yourself will be clouded, ignorant, subjective opinions and attitudes. And if that should happen, dear listeners, well then I should be wasting my time speaking to you for it is my hope and desire that you form in your minds and come to, a friendly and impartial judgement regarding what I have said to you in the openness of my mind and the honesty of my heart and soul. So there. Heed to my words and I will not be wasting either my own time or yours''.

★   ★   ★

At this stage there was a long silence and we all began to wonder what had become of our guest and his interesting tale. Not as much as a whisper could be heard from the place, situated somewhere above our heads and right central over the table where the voice had been speaking. After what seemed like an hour but which was probably only about three minutes or so, we heard him again.

''Before I continue and tell you of the interesting things that succeeded my remedying the fault and mounting up to go away again, I have decided that it would be better if we took a break here for approximately fifteen minutes. So if ye will just excuse me, I'm sure you will welcome a moment of relaxation.''

# Chapter Three

While our guest was busying himself with whatever he was up to, we all stood up from the table and stretched our legs. Some assiduous person made up a brew of tea which we all sipped gratefully and with little talk. Hardly any reference was made to the story we were hearing and most of the mumbles and comments were directed to the stiff knees and sore joints obtained through sitting still for a long period of time. We were all back in our places, tea finished, when we heard him again.

"After what could be estimated to be three and a half days of travelling through land that was both lonely and wild, sustained by a diet of berries and hazel nuts with the dessert of an odd sweet chestnut, as luck would have me find that particular tree, and keeping my mount in shape with the good juices of Irish grass, a sharp awareness of the senses and a keen vigilance of mind had established themselves in my nature. I knew many things I had never known before. For instance, that when the moon shines it reveals to the wary eye all the strange and nebulous things which dwell in the air around us but which are not apparent at first glance or in ordinary light. I could describe these things to you if you want me to. Let me say that they are the nightly manifestations, or shadows as it were, of things which can be seen in even greater vivacity and detail by the rays of the brightly shining noon sun. At night, they gyrate and hop against the milk-pale light. Their outer parts merge into the shadows. At noon, if and when the sun is at its best, along the edges of the rays, where the light mixes in a multitude of unbelievable colours and funny hazes, one can see them groping and flickering, trying, as it were, to leap away from whatever was holding them back and head in liberated ecstasy to be swallowed up in the sun. At some moments they can be quite appealing to the eye but more often than not I have felt frightened by them. I wonder do they know of my presence or are they oblivious to everything around them. What are they? Where do they come from? What is their purpose?

Another revelation concerned the noises of the dark hours. Naturally, they are not those of the day when the normal, accepted, visible things go about their business. They are different. Mention has already been made of the fact that sounds of any kind are rare in the nocturnal hours in that land. Oh indeed you will hear the wind sigh and the branches sway and the leaves whisper but that is about all; no chorus of unknown creatures or mysterious echoes.

Well that is the case for unpractised ears. I was fooled in the beginning. Now I know differently. The silence is a kind of cover, not a deliberate one I suppose, for the very intense nightly activities which go on in the shadows. And these goings on make quite a loud racket. You can hear it if you listen carefully and closely and learn to decipher the tones through the silence. Behind the wall of natural quietness I could hear a hum of busied activity. It goes on everywhere in the country. At some places it is of a greater intensity that at others, reflecting no doubt a higher concentration of whatever it is that causes the noise. It has been impossible for me to deduce from what I hear the exact nature of what goes on. It could be anything. Anything at all.

Sometimes a peculiar noise which resembles a vast horde of beings singing and dancing at one moment, and a terrible fight with all manners of noisy weapons being used at another, comes from all around and when I compare it with the peaceful silence that can be heard through the opposite ear, it becomes quite worrying. May Fortune protect and save us. That is a prayer that was on my lips many a time.

These noises were most obvious when the pace of my horse was slow and even. After a while I had given up all efforts at hurrying, as there was no place I was hurrying to. Most of the time now I was just pacing along at a snail's pace. The horse was quite content to walk and so was I. Sometimes I would doze off and if you ask me, the horse did too for many's the time he had to be redirected away from a thick clump of trees or a river's edge and more than once I awoke to find us stranded in some mire or bog. We were getting used to each other's ways and there was little or no antagonism between us. Remember what I told you earlier on about me discovering an intense dislike for people in me that I never had thought was there? It was more apparent now that I had become solitary. I purposefully dodged or avoided or simply ignored any humans happening along the itinerary. Well, for quite a long time now the journey had been pleasant as not one single individual had happened to come along. It was as if there were no people left at all in the wide world. I was happy.

Imagine the irritation and vexation that struck me when I discovered that there was somebody coming along behind me and to top it all off, he was intent on following my trail. I estimated the person, who also was on a horse, to be about half an Irish mile behind. He was so careless in hiding his presence that there existed little difficulty in hearing his every move and step. Whenever my nag stopped for a quick drink or a swift bite of fresh grass, the one behind would stop too, only to start off once again when we had. I was raging.

Ahead of us, along by the side of the track, was a notice nailed to the low hanging bow of an oak. When I came up close it was possible to read it. It said:

"CHOIG MAINISTER NAOMH PADRAIC".

For the benefit of foreigners that translates as:

"TO THE MONASTERY OF SAINT PATRICK".

A small arrow pointed the way into the foliage.

True enough, between the bushes and branches was a dark monastery with heavy smoke coming out of a chimney. It was a tall building and curiously enough in this land of wood and timber, it was made of solid stone. It is hard to conceive of where they could have got that stone. The windows were the usual narrow slit affairs, through which it was easier to see out than to see in. Normally I would have gone right past that place. There was no desire in me to meet and listen to anybody, whether they be common labourers or monks. An even greater annoyance however would be to have to continue along the way with that person following me. I could kill two birds with one stone by stopping off at the monastery. It would be possible to see the rider as he passed by, thinking I was ahead of him and then it would be easier for me to decide if he were a friend or foe. A short stop in my journey would also enable me to have a drink, and a relaxation, especially for my behind. I'm sure that the horse would not have said no to a stop either.

I swiftly turned in off the roadway and then dismounted silently in the bushes. The pathway up to the monastery was narrow and badly overgrown with scrub. It was not that it was seldom used, for it was well-trodden and had a foot-worn hollow extending right to the door and which was a good twelve inches below the level of the surrounding ground; it was just that nobody ever took any care of it, leaving it to the tender mercy of the weed and thorn. From what I know of monks and that kind of clergy in general, the wild, unkempt pathway probably had some religious significance. There was a tree at the front of the building which seemed to be ideal to tie a horse to. This I did. A clear view of the nag's face was available, for the first time. His eyes were red and hot and his mouth was open and foaming. His breathing was a bit laboured. I didn't know that he was so tired. Well, the rest would do him good. We had a long way to go yet and it occurred to me that I might have to get a sharp riding whip for the horse was looking at me now with rebellious and not too friendly eyes.

The heavy wooden door was opened almost immediately to my knocking. A monk invited me inside. There were a number of people sitting around at tables. Most were monks though there were some of the laity. Labourers most of the latter were, I would say. In one corner was a bar. A person who I'd say was a monk but who had on a white shirt with the sleeves rolled up was behind the counter. The whole scene was lit by means of rather ancient oil lamps. That would be vegetable oil, let me say, and not the modern variety. I was escorted to the bar and then promptly abandoned. I asked for a mug of beer, barley beer, a strong brew that everybody drank at that time and this was immediately placed before me. As I sipped long, thirsty draughts the window aperture gave me a view of the external world and in particular, the roadway beyond, along which my friend, if he were so, would soon be coming.

"Ah my good man, And where would you have come from now and where at all at all would the grace of God be taking you to?" The inquisitor was a clerical gentleman who had sidled up to me almost without my noticing. I did not like his bossy, big head.

I didn't answer, but just kept looking out the window, as if he was not there.

"We get many people coming in here to visit us. Friends and strangers, from all parts of the world. We had a visitor from Constantinople once, believe it or not. He was a poor wayfarer, looking for gold and treasure. I told him that he would never find any in this country, so he went back home again to his relatives and friends where he belonged. Many other people too, I may assure you, have had their lives changed by just calling in here and speaking to me. What are you looking for, my son?"

"Nothing, father. Nothing at all."

"Oh come now, come now. We are all looking for something in this life, aren't we?"

"I have everything I want," Fada found himself saying, involuntarily, for he had no wish to pursue a conversation of any kind.

"I wish he would hurry up so I can see who he is," Fada muttered to himself. "What? What is that you said?" inquired the monk, straining closer.

Fada was feeling a bit affected by the ale. It was a stronger brew in those days. He became almost oblivious to the monk and his whole surroundings in general. He was only faintly aware of their presence, or of any presence at all, as he continued to gaze out the window, itself becoming a task of strain. Fortitude, patience, wit and bravery, an even temper, moderation; no rage, vengeance, jealousy, small-mindedness – that was to be the blueprint for Fada's character in all cases now, as it had been in the past. And it should not be a very difficult standard to attain. For was there not the example set by –."

★　★　★

Now for the first time there was an interruption in the proceedings, much to my chagrin. The indication I got that somebody was disturbed was a banging on the table and loud, voluntary coughing. This upset everything, for Fada had stopped speaking in the middle of a sentence. I looked for the interrupter and felt very annoyed. It was a stout, middle-aged man.

"What is it?" I asked him between my teeth.

"He's talking in the third person."

"Who is?" I asked, not having a clue at first what he was referring to.

"Our guest. Fada MacCarthaig."

"So?"

"It is very strange. Do you think that he is genuine? That he is telling the truth?"

"And why, for whatever imaginable reason under the sun do you think that he might want to spin us a yarn of lies? Do you think a person like him who has lived a full life and who has watched the progress of human existence for centuries and centuries would waste his time leading us into airy-fairy land just for the sake of it? Do you now?"

"No. I guess not."

"May I continue?" It was Fada back again, to my relief.

★   ★   ★

"Ah. I have heard that said before. It is a statement that has come from many a mouth and one which everyone, who has ever said it, has lived to retract." The monk was obviously intent on getting his point over to me. One had to admire his persistence.

"Are you a criminal?", he then asked.

"Are you?" I replied.

"Don't you show disrespect please."

"An honest question deserves an honest answer."

"I have your welfare at heart my son."

"There is somebody coming up the road," I uttered in a burst of excitement.

With my much sharpened sense of hearing it was possible for me to hear the rider approaching. I could even estimate him to be exactly one hundred horse-paces down. Then the thought shook me. Would he see the sign outside this place and come in? If he did, then I would have little opportunity to defend myself against him in whatever way was necessary. I would also have lost the chance to catch him out by surprise. I hoped that he would go on right past and then I could go out and follow him.

Between the trees the shape of a horse and rider were flashing by. Their speed was steady and it was difficult to see them clearly through the trunks and branches. In a short clearing almost directly in my line of view it was possible to see more clearly. I concentrated my gaze on this spot. Then they passed. It was Sean Og. The sliveen. A most annoying nephew of mine. Worse than that. A sneaking, conniving good for nothing for whom I never had any time.

He went past without as much as looking in the direction of the monastery. It took me some time to assimilate what I had seen. That this nephew whom I and everybody else to the best of my knowledge, detested and who was also never left in any doubt as to his standing in my books, that he should be FOLLOWING ME.

I didn't know what to think.

"The WRETCH," I shouted out.

"Is he a friend of yours?" asked the monk.

"May I ask you a question?" I asked him, quietly.

"That is what I am here for," he replied, in a gentle voice.

"Is murder ever justified? Ever? A direct answer now."

"Well now, no question, and especially one like that, can be always answered with a straight yes or no. I . . ."

I broke him off in mid-sentence.

"Are you going to answer my question or not?"

"Well, the most direct answer I can give you is, yes. Sometimes it is justifiable for one person to take another's life. But - - -."

"THANK YOU, THANK YOU", I shouted at him. "In that case I am going to throttle that little runt out there and also take the greatest pleasure in doing it. Thank you father for your advice."

With that I dropped my now empty mug and dashed for the door.

"Wait. Come back. I must tell you something". It was the monk shouting out.

I didn't wait. Very quickly, I pulled the latch and went outside to the horse. A moment later we were away, with the sound of the monk's voice shouting something I wasn't able to make out, sailing through the air and becoming lost in the whistling and blowing of the wind.

After ten minutes, the sight of the nephew ahead came into view. A depressing, annoying, humiliating sight.

He was the illegitimate son of my now dead sister. Goodness knows who his father was.

I was puzzled to know what he could want; what he thought he might get from me. The sight of his thin, stick-like frame, almost out of view in the coat he was wearing, brought a feeling of morbid pity along with disgust to me.

I quickened my pace and went up to him.

The sight of his face immediately destroyed that emotion of pity, meagre as it was, and an almost uncontrollable fury came over me. It was a while before I could speak.

"What is it? What do you want?," I demanded.

He gave a weak, insipid smile.

"Hello Uncle," was all he replied.

"Suffering snakes. May the gods of sticks and stones look down on us. Why have you followed me?"

"Uncle. I was thinking about you all the time and wondering what had become of you. After all, I am one of your closest relatives and I am interested in everything you do."

This lad always spoke in slow, dreary monosyllables and the impression he gave in his speech, as in everything else, was one of deep insincerity. Even his thin, sly strands of cunning brownish hair seemed to suit him!

"I only want to talk to you and accompany you along the way. You won't be lonely then, will you?"

I was at a loss for words to answer him.

"Ah Uncle. For a man of your age and dignity to take up the life of a wanderer is bitter sauce indeed. They all wonder about you at home, thinking you have taken to the bottle. But I guessed better of you and thought that you had more magnanimous plans afoot. Would I be wrong in making such a salutary and creditable conclusion?"

"Magnanimous plans? Magnanimous plans afoot indeed, how are you. And what sort of plan do you think I might possibly have in my head now?"

"Uncle. Do you know that you do not look very rested? I think that it would be a good idea if you took a nap and left me to watch over everything. You could sleep relaxed, in the knowledge that everything was in safe hands." It was then that I suddenly realized he was sneaking swift glances in the direction of my saddle where my property, including the bag, was. At first I thought this was just due to the shifty nature which was a part of his eyes, as of his whole being. Then I contemplated the gift of gold I had received from the venerables back home and realized that the supposed nephew could have knowledge of it. A grin of satisfaction and sarcasm I could hardly suppress.

This half-grin, accompanied by a deep gurgle, was followed by a feeling of the utmost despair and outrage that I should be encumbered with the cross of his presence. I felt as if I was being suffocated and strangled at one and the same time. It was a desperate feeling. My mind became completely clouded with ideas of violence and all manner of pictures. Some of these pictures or visions were bad and extremely vicious and, you know, they actually had the power to put me off too. I was a bit scared myself. I remembered what had happened in previous instances when such emotions had got out of hand and I tried to control myself. Not only was there a loathing to add to the total of people who had already fallen foul of my goodwill and paid severely for it with their lives, but there also was a loathing in me to take the life of a blood relation, even though I considered him a pretty remote relative, due to the anonymity of his father. There is a strong tradition in our culture that you must not murder a blood relative. And strangely enough, this applies with particular emphasis to rather distant relations. It seems that the more far apart they are from you in the matter of blood, the more sombre it is to do away with them. However, if it is your mother or son then the matter is more forgiveable. We are a strange breed of people indeed and the time spent in this other world and all I have seen has done nothing to contradict that conclusion.

A more worthy and better idea would be to just simply lose the lad somewhere. In the countryside we were in it would not be a difficult thing to do. The whole place was full of trees and bushes. Indeed all Ireland appeared to be apparalled in woods. I never knew this before. I had imagined all manner of strange landscapes and wonderous sights to lie beyond the hills and beyond our ken. Now it was discovered that the whole country was made of just the same old timber and plants. I felt, when I thought on it, as if I was travelling in an extended back garden which somebody had neglected and that when I came out of it, I would be merely at the other side of my home baile. In other words, it was as if I was going nowhere. Nowadays of course, all this has been studied and classified under the heading of Einstein's Relativity. Travel and direction do not exist and this is made apparent even to the uneducated eye (as mine was), especially when the places one is supposed to be travelling through is the same place all the time. That is how the theory became familiar to me without having to take any notes or put any thought into it whatsoever.

Anyway, I suppose you are all getting tired of these little philosophical observations of mine making me appear like a very wise man just because I have lived before and know most of what there is to know.

What you want to hear about is what happened to the nephew and what about Amerigo Vespucci and my adventures with him.

It was not as easy to get rid of the chap in the trees and bushes at all. Not as easy as one would have thought. I said to him–

"Stay there a minute while I take my horse and myself into the bushes for to go to the toilet and don't budge from that spot afear we never meet again."

But a long time later when I re-emerged from out the hedge quite a distance from where I originally left the trail, who should be there but my nephew. I still do not know how he could have possibly managed to follow me along while I and the nag plugged our way through the undergrowth. A veritably impossible task one would imagine. But apparently it was not beyond me oul sogocia.

"Everybody at home was asking for you", he said this time, as if realising he was in my bad books and trying to improve his standing with me.

"How far are you intending to come with me?", I asked him. He chose to ignore the question.

"That horse of your's is not a bad creature. Where did you get him?"

His question made me rage. The sneaky rat. Why did he ask such a question if he didn't mean to catch me out? I thought a long while before I answered. I thought about him and studied his face closely. I thought about his rearing and childhood. I tried to think of bad stories I had heard about him. They were plentiful and all had one standing-out quality; the underhandedness of his deeds. Then I tried to apply all this to the present situation. There was a conclusion staring me in the face. He was out to blackmail me. First of all he would discover something I did that some people would consider illegal and then he would face me with his knowledge of my so-called guilt.

Then he would demand something from me in return for silence. What? The bag I had put the gold in of course.

"I bought him from a gypsy," was my clear answer.

"He was a bargain," I added, to give my answer the weight of credibility

"He sure looks like a fine one. A nice hindquarters. It's time to rest, Uncle. The sun is down, the sky is blackening and you look tired out."

"I appreciate your concern," I replied sarcastically.

So there we lay the two of us on the thorny scrub staring up at the bleak sky. There was not a comfort to be found anywhere, in the sky, the land, the company. That individual had a most persistent natter and he also had the knack, which is exclusive to bores, of being able to prevent the listener from getting a word in edgeways. I didn't mind his senseless chattering for it was one way of keeping awake. I had no intention of closing my eyes while he was about. I would sit the night out.

But then I began to feel drowsy and almost as if I was being hypnotised. So that was his game.

To make me drop off with his ceaseless drone.

I should have watched out for such a trick. The brat.

"Shut up with your talk. Be quiet immediately. I'll have no more of it."

And he stopped talking, if you could call it that, and went straight off to sleep. Or I think he did. He was soon snoring, or pretending to. Come early morning while it was still fairly dark and, almost sure he was fast asleep, I got up and went to my nag. I had to wake him up!

My tired, courageous mount came to, without as much as a grunt.

"Where are you going, Uncle?"

The words came as I was mounting, with one leg almost over.

★   ★   ★

Through the wet, rainy land we plied our way. Sometimes the sun would show itself from out of behind the rain-clouds and bathe us in its faint warmth. In sunlight one felt more lighthearted and had a tendency to smile and laugh at little things, and ignore all the headaches. It was during these bright periods that the freedom that was associated with my new way of life was most intensely felt and enjoyed. Once I actually joked with Sean Og. It was on impulse. My nag was dragging a bit and sweating.

"I'd exchange this nag for a hag any time," I said lightheartedly.

By the way, a hag is a woman. Let Fada continue.

"You'd like to exchange your nag for a hag? Why? She'd never get you there in time like a horse would. Anyway, I thought you always hated women."

"She might not get me there in time," I laughed, "but she would make a more pleasant horse!"

★　★　★

I was soon sick of Sean Og again for he had nothing of any interest to say. My chance came just before we were about to round a bend. He said that he wanted to stop for a moment, and dismounted to relieve himself at the side. When he was in the middle of this act, I walloped the behind of my mount and went helterskelter around the corner. I kept going at a fantastic speed. By the time the next corner had been reached there was still no sign of your man coming round the first bend. It was a great feeling I had then. Just to be free of his company for a moment was a blessed relief. But how long would it be before he'd catch up again? It was sure to happen. I set my mind working on this. I chewed it over for a considerable period of time, maintaining all the while a quick gallop.

At last a great idea struck me. A brilliant plan. It was this.

At the side as I went by were large numbers of massive oak trees, standing like giant, bearded sentries. I thought of a sudden that these trees could be put to a use. I quickly dismounted. Now no man in those days ever went travelling without an axe. Attached to the saddle was such an instrument, with a short handle. Immediately the axe was set to work on a huge oak and in no time at all a huge bite was cut into it. The poor tree began to creak. For a moment my heart stood still for I thought it was about to go. Then a sturdy piece of stick was inserted in the bite, like as if it were holding apart a shark's jaws. I continued to chop away at the wood; soon it was almost eaten through and was just about ready to fall. In fact all its weight now rested on that piece of stick. Maybe now you can see what I was up to. A piece of handy rope was tied to the safety stick and, making sure it was slack, I went with the other end of it into the bushes and hid myself with my horse. I pitied the poor amadan as he came up the road, humming to himself and looking as if he hadn't a care in the world. Soon he was near to the fatal spot. Would you believe it? I could hear the oak creaking and it was making a terrible racket. Your man stopped and cocked his ear, listening. He was just a few feet from the tree. There was complete silence in the forest, except for the creaking. It was as if all the animals and birds had flown from the vicinity.

At last he moved forward again and I pulled the rope.

There was an almighty crack and I heard a horrible scream, presumably the nephew's. I looked up to the top of the tree with satisfaction. Imagine how I felt when I saw it falling my way. The massive mountain of trunk, branches and leaves was hurtling down towards me. The noise it was making would be difficult to describe accurately. It was like a hurricane (many of which I was to experience later), a mixture of thunder and wind with showers of dirt and twigs coming down first. The sun appeared to be flickering and disappearing behind it.

Before I closed my eyes I had a quick look at Sean Og. He was standing as stiff as a statue, his mouth wide open, staring skywards at the falling giant.

The ground shook all round me like an earthquake. My feet left the ground and I rose into the air, returning again to my former standing position. By a miracle the tree trunk had missed by inches. I had been in the fork of branch and trunk.

The rascal was all sympathy and advice.

"God is with you. You stand high in His eyes," he was saying. Then, as we prepared to mount, he came up with a real cute one.

"Uncle Fada," he intoned, looking at my saddle bag, "both you and your nag have had a big shock. Look at his eyes and nostrils. He is terrified. Let me make life easier for both of you. I will carry your saddle bag."

"You will not carry anything. You would be better off tailing back home as where I am going could be of no possible interest to you. In fact I'm sure you will only too gladly leave my company soon. So why not save yourself trouble and go back now?"

"I will stay with you just a while longer and then I will go," he answered.

He smiled at me and then said:

"It does one good to get away from BaileMacCarthaig once in a while, doesn't it?"

Instead of answering him, I just hit my nag and got it going in a swift trot.

Well, it is true that most of the time we were seeing nothing but wood and bush. Although we were treading the main highway northwards, oftentimes it was necessary to cut through bramble or leap obstacles. And, contrary to expectations, the further north we went the worse did the civilisation seem to become. It became more savage. This fact was now becoming plain. After a long time on the road, we were well out of our own province and in strange country. Naturally I did my best to avoid people whenever possible, despite the inane appeals of Sean Og. He kept saying, let's go in to that house, or, let's talk to that fellow, or, look Uncle, do you think that old man (or lady) might be carrying valuables?

All along he was on the lookout for easy pickings. But it was my intention to keep out of all possible trouble. Whenever somebody was seen, or heard coming in the distance, we hid ourselves in the trees. Only when they had safely gone past would we reappear. This was surely a wise policy in what to us was alien country. For now, more frequently than before, we were coming upon armed bands of men, looking very fierce. Whenever we saw them coming, the nephew was always the first into the bush.

I could see him getting more nervous now. It was the strange country and the signs of warfare that was causing it. He did not talk as much as he used to and was jumpy. I must admit myself that there was an uneasiness in my bones, especially when we began to come upon towns which had been attacked and burned down. We always skirted these. Now Sean Og obeyed me in everything and stuck to me like a frightened puppy. After a while it became extremely irritating to have to dodge these columns of men, who sometimes were on horseback and sometimes on foot. We were making very slow progress and it was all very hard on the nerves.

Eventually we came across an actual battle. Two bodies of men were fighting in front of the gates of a walled town. They were using swords, spears, axes, pikes, clubs and some huge men were swinging large metal balls which, whenever they hit anybody, knocked their heads off. It was hard to see how they could avoid hitting their own men for the two sides (or maybe three) were closely interlocked. At a distance from these another part of the fight was in progress. There were men on horseback charging each other. They were all shouting and yelling and they wore ragged clothes. Nobody wore armour then. As they charged, they aimed long sticks at their adversary, the ends of which had been sharpened into long points. We did not wait to see the outcome of the war. All in all, it was a very imposing sight and a much more sophisticated affair than what we were used to at home.

Towns, villages and citizens were becoming very numerous now.

The people were all wearing fancy clothes and their hair was so short that sometimes it did not even cover their ears. I would not want to talk to any of them. I can just imagine what their superior attitude would be to us country people. Insults would pour out, even through their eyes if their mouths were shut. They would claim to be very civilised and so forth, and I'm sure it would be difficult to understand what they were saying, even though it would be in my own language. At last, and against my better judgement, conversation was entered into with one of these metropolitans. I wanted to find the correct direction to BaileAthaCliath.

"BlathCliath ansuth," he said in a wheezy voice.

"What?" I shouted, mystified and frightened by what he'd said.

"He says we're here," said the nephew, with a smile.

"Thank you," I said sarcastically to the nephew.

"You are both from the country I see. What brings ye to our fair city on this holy day, may I ask?"

"I have heard so much about your great city I just had to come and see it," I said lyingly.

"Well, what do you think now?", he asked.

"I think that where we are from the people are more civilised. I have never seen so much blood spilt and in such vicious ways as on my way to this place. It is a disgrace on the fair name of the land. If people outside this country ever come to hear of this behaviour they will write off the Gael as an untamable savage. And worse."

"You will find that we behave differently in the confines of this city."

"Do you know of any nice place we might be able to put up for a while? Not too expensive." It was the nephew speaking.

The man, an old fellow in a strange looking outfit, thought a while and then said:

"In Moore's street there is a house belonging to Mr O'Byrne. It is very suitable. Ask for number four."

"We will do that surely. Thank you indeed for your very appreciated help."

I was glad that the fellow had not turned out to be too awkward. When we had set ourselves up in Mr. O'Byrne's place, I began to make my plans. When the candles were all out and the room and city was in darkness, I lay back, my head resting on my joined hands.

"Where are you going in the morning?", asked Sean Og.

I coughed to clear my throat.

"I'm going to the Aras where they keep the coaches and then I'm going on a long journey to Donegal. You are not coming with me."

The young fellow stayed very quiet after this and I soon fell off to sleep. Came early morning and Sean was still dozing. Or so he pretended to be. I put on my bare clothes and prepared myself for the day ahead. I washed my face and feet and brushed my shaggy hair and beard. Whether Sean Og heard me or not I didn't care, for everything was thought out. Then downstairs quickly with me and out the door. The nags were there, and they looked at me with their ungrateful hot eyes.

"You'll soon be rid of me and I of you, you lazy donkeys."

Leading my own one out, I met a citizen in the alleyway. To his obvious surprise, he was offered the free gift of one horse.

"I am going on a large ship instead," I said, "a long ways."

He took the reins and ran away with the nag down the alleyway.

Then inside with me again and into a small room that was used to store things. Here I settled down comfortably and waited.

My wait lasted as long as a dog's bark.

Upstairs I heard loud noises and the shuffling of feet. A door was opened in a rough manner and somebody ran out into the yard. A loud crack filled the air and it seemed as if his nag had started off in a gallop, without the intermediary of a walk, slow trot quickening into a properly controlled gallop. I hoped that be would break his neck.

★   ★   ★

Many hours later I was on the seafront and there I saw a large ship. It was the first ocean-going vessel I had ever seen and it looked like a mountain. High up were the huge white sails blowing like giant tents. A spirit of adventure filled me.

The man in charge told me that it would cost three ounces of gold and one ounce of silver (or alternatively, five ounces of gold – this struck me as a strange sense of value, gold being more valuable than silver – but I took him at his word) to go to where the ship was headed.

"And what is the name of the place?", I enquired.

"They call it France now."

"All right. I will go there."

Some hours later we were sailing out on to the wide, vast, lonely, dark and immense ocean.

All the while I felt myself getting smaller and smaller till at length I was sure I was on the verge of disappearing.

The captain helped me to my bed and gave me a strong brew to, as he put it, "tide you over".

# Chapter Four

If you are a person who thinks that mankind improves in different countries and that people are more civilised there, you have another think coming. I had no sooner alighted from the ship and said goodbye to the whole crew, than I was met with a hail of stones from ignorant roughnecks. I could not understand what it was they were saying and I gave them a piece of my own mind in the Irish tongue. I had this kind of trouble all the way to Paris for which I was headed. My face and body had taken such a battering that by the time the great city had been reached, I was a mass of bruises and blood and I was taken to a hospital. Here it was nice and relaxing despite the operations and the treatment I had to undergo. There was no ether for putting a patient to sleep in those days so, instead, they forced me to drink a very strong spirit and I would end up completely unconscious. A total of two months was spent in that place. Before I left, they gave me a farewell party for I seemed to have become very popular.

"In France we have a very strict culture you know. Every person is in his or her place and one must always be capable of distinguishing between different people."

"How is that?", I asked. Pierre was a friend who wanted me to work for him.

"Well it all started some time back. As you must be aware, France once ruled over an empire that encompassed the whole world. This was a better empire than the empire of the Romans."

"Who are they?"

"They were the Italians."

"They were. I find your talk interesting and of much benefit to me. Go on."

"O my dear, dear Pierre . . . ."

A female he knew had interrupted. Her purring voice was like that of a cat, and it was to become familiar to me over the course of the next few days.

"Andree. Meet my friend Fada. He is from Ireland."

She came over to me and before I knew what was happening she was stroking my beard. She and Pierre were talking and laughing at the same time in their own tongue.

"She likes you. She finds your beard a happy sight."

"She does?" I said, not knowing what to think.

Our conversation was resumed with the hag sitting on his knee.

"Soon however, a new group of people infused themselves into our way of life. We were glad to have them and it was our greatest victory ever. We called them the Indians. It was all right at first and then a bit of prejudice grew up in the provinces and they were called Gypsies. Later still, they came to Paris and now they are called Parisians. They brought their own way of life and customs with them and they have passed these on. Among them are the strict caste system, the accordian and the Muslim religion. This is our French history."

We sipped wine which lightened my mind and I listened with some wonder.

"What are you?," I asked him in the end in a questioning tone.

"I am a monarchist. France and the king are one. Many people have not seen that yet. But they will."

"If you are an ambitious man, as you say you are, why do you spend your days hanging around this flea-bitten saloon? Why are you not in politics putting all your ideas and plans into practice?"

"In France we do things not as they do them elsewhere. This is something which I am trying to teach you. I have more influence on the course of history by sitting here than I would have in the hallowed chambers of parliament; so I believe. It has long been shown by the great dramatists how the quiet and cunning came to the throne while the ones who thought they were making the running only got the back seat in the end. One day a call will come to me in this place and sorrowfully, I will leave my humble ways and go on to higher things."

When he had finished talking he laughed very loudly and hit the girl across her knees.

She laughed too but I think that slap hurt her because her legs had gone all red. She rubbed them and also darted a little smile at me. This attempt at seduction was ignored on my part. When they talked in French, I picked up odd words here and there and in this way, I was learning the language of the French. I didn't know what to expect next from the two of them; they were joking and gesticulating all the time. Then Pierre excused himself and with the most fancy of leaps as I've ever seen, went over the balcony and vanished.

Her ladyship smiled at me. She came over and sat on a stool at my side. She fixed herself comfortably and had to look up at me, as the stool was much lower down. Her clothes were loose-fitting and her hair was long and colourful. She spoke in French and she also used sign-language. It was the most exhausting conversation I have ever had.

"Is your mummy dead?", she asked in a consoling tone of voice.

"She died having me," was my proud reply.

"Oh that is a terrible thing, to have no mummy," she wailed.

To put her at her ease, I told her about Aine who had been a mother to me.

"She is my grandaunt and she was better than a mother to me. I promised her that I would make a petition in her name in the Holy City of Rome when I get there".

This revelation to the woman that I was not completely alone in the world did not seem to satisfy her, for the next thing she was grabbing my sleeve and shouting:

"No, do not go there. Rome is a wicked city and the people are only half civilised. Please promise me that you won't go," she pleaded protectively.

The thought ran through my head that this lady was not one to whom virtue was a virtue, and that she was trying to interfere in my affairs as no woman ever should; and that she was trying to order my life for me. But I kept this thought quiet for a while.

"Woman," I said to her sternly, at the same time disengaging my arm from her grip;

"I am a wandering Gael; a man of the open road who loves the sky before anything on earth. It's in my blood."

When I said those words she suddenly transferred herself from the stool to a sitting position on my lap. Needless to say, I was momentarily astounded.

"I know more about you than you do yourself," she whispered into my ear, so that I could feel her breath there.

These remarks of her's I did not like. I was thinking that she was too uppity for a wench, and I could not make out what her meanings were.

"Not even Aunt Aine knew everything about me," I told her.

"Is that so? You stupid men know nothing about the power of us womenfolk. Come here my ugly one."

She put her arms around my neck and kissed me on the gob. Then she began feeling my ears, something not even my late, dear departed betrothed Pegeen dared attempt to do. She also pinched me in various spots and squeezed me as tight as a bear. In walked your man at that very moment and sees us like that. Naturally I was glad, but herself just let out a few swear words, got up and left the room without a word and in a huff. Just as she got to the door she gave a hell of a dirty look to your man and then she winked at me.

With utter contempt and disgust I waved her out.

"It is lucky you came in when you did," I said to Pierre, "for I was just about to hit her good and hard."

He looked at me queerly and without a word produced a document from out of his pocket.

"This is a contract which comes the way of people who are in some way uniquely blessed. Needless to say, you are one of those, having come all the way here from Ireland, and having told such a story about your killings. The Arabs over in the near East, Asia of the Spices – perfumed nights of a thousand kisses – nothing like it – it is where I spent my youth – require men from foreign lands to help them with their enterprises. They pay out of this world. It is a token of my esteem for you that I ask you to sign this contract at the bottom of the page. It is written in Arabic but I can translate it for you."

"How will I get there?", I asked.

"Have you ever heard of the magic flying carpets?", was his strange question.

"No, I have not." At that time there were many things I didn't know.

"Well in actual fact, for unusual reasons, you won't remember anything of the journey for it is their custom to put their people into a special blessed sleep, so you will be there before you know it. What you will not immediately realise is that you will have been transported there on a magic carpet."

"May the Power and Fortune protect us. It is scarcely believable."

Outside the life of the city was going its way, a babble of voices, carts and stomping animals, market women and bells. A chorus of song was flowing into the room and next door was the sound of the drinkers. A sudden look of pain came over Pierre and he pulled a long dagger from his inside, and pointed it at me.

"It is quite possible that certain jealous parties may attempt to hinder your progress and they could even come here to try and kidnap you. Sign the paper quickly and do exactly as I say. One false move and I may have to use this dagger. Do you understand?"

I signed the paper and with the dagger in my back for protection I went out and down a passage to another room. As I went into a small dark chamber I spied Andree peeping at me behind a corner."

★　★　★

At this stage in our proceedings Fada's voice trailed away, and us assembled lot were left looking at each other.

"A most interesting tale. It has the ring of truth," said one.

"This is the first time I have had such clear communication with the nether world," I informed them.

The tea was again being diligently prepared by the ladies present and the homely whistle of the kettle on the hob was heard by all. A comfortable feeling pervaded the room. Conversation was minimal and extremely restrained.

Before we resumed, I suggested that everybody sit in a different seat this time to improve concentration. Outside, the stars still twinkled.

"I hope he comes back in time," whined one man whom I noticed was a complainer. I don't know what he was doing there at all.

"He'll be back. He hasn't let us down yet, has he?", said another.

"I wish I could get some sleep, I'm exhausted," said one lady, her face pale.

"You will, soon," I assured her, "but you wouldn't want to miss the experience of a lifetime, would you?"

Most were quiet, only their breathing and the odd sigh being noticeable. Resignation was evident.

"Andree was a funny girl. She was out tapping at my door one night and whispering for me to let her in. Violent feelings of hatred and nausea filled me as I guessed her intention. The next morning they found Pierre stabbed to death and herself missing. They figured it was herself who was responsible. Nobody knew why she had done such a terrible thing. Of course the plans for my future were finished now. How can I describe myself, and my feelings as I walked by the bank of the Seine that afternoon? I had now taken over the running of Pierre's place. Some dark-skinned fellow had approached me and informed me it was now my duty to do so until further notice. He said he was a relative of Pierre but he certainly didn't look like him. So in a way material security had come to me, uninvited as it were. But I felt terribly insecure. I didn't recognise myself as the man I was yesterday and violent feelings kept coming to me. Whenever an oaf made an obstruction of himself (or herself, may I add, for a distinction between what they call the sexes had never been to my liking), that oaf was promptly deposited with a good elbow to that part of the byway where he or she rightly belonged.

"AND QUITE OFTEN THIS INVOLVED ALSO A CHANGE FROM THE VERTICAL TO THE HORIZONTAL POSITION," Fada thundered, and his voice was like a storm in the room, scaring the guests and astonishing even me, normally an imperturbable individual. At this stage, I said, I would like to go into my own attributes, as a comparison of them with those of our narrator in chief, Fada, would be interesting, for in some queer way I feel responsible for Fada, for having dragged him up from the dead; so that perhaps there is a feeling of guilt there on my part, or maybe, stretching the imagination a good deal now, mind you, maybe he is a distant ancestor of mine. I sometimes too feel that kind of insecurity Fada mentions, so that often I don't know who I am.

I related some personal details and characteristics to the frightened people, hoping to put their minds at rest with a bit of an explanation. It is amazing how easy it is for people to become frightened. Especially when there is absolutely nothing to be frightened about.

Fada resumed in a quieter voice. "In my thinking, as I travelled the bank of the river, an urge to accomplish something and to become famous filled me, and set me thinking. But what could I become famous for? What had I done and what could I do; these were questions that filled my thinking. They became an obsession with me, the how and the wherefore. I thought on what I was personally capable of performing, in the matter of feats, and I realised there was very little. There was, however, my ability to consume large amounts of porter, and from my observation here I don't think there was any talent in that field to be found in the whole city. Suppose, I pondered, I held an exhibition of my putting the porter back or held a competition with the natives, my fame might then spread. Then I thought back to the time I was a youngster and did a feat at the local Feis and won great applause. Would that astonish them here, I thought, would it make their eyes pop with wonder? Or would the ability to do this still be with me after multiple years of neglect? It is called the "Lame" and is very unusual. Shortly I will describe what ensued.

It was at this juncture, walking by the river, that I met the philosopher Pedro, whom I have already mentioned. A great fellow. But at first he was a bit surprising. I spotted him crouching behind a riverside bush at my approach. He was barely distinguishable from the leaves, a well-camouflaged figure. Why he was hiding at my coming is another question; he said it was due to the play of the dusk light on my back, producing a mirage of a giant image; but I suspect it was really a weakness in his own character that made him the way he was.

I walked by the bush and grabbed him by the hair of his head. He received a sound thrashing delivered in a felicitous manner. I doubt very much whether his frail frame would have survived the evening had not fifty-one Parisians taken pity on his wails and forced me to desist.

"It is all right," I calmed them down, "he is my son and I love him. It is all for his own good."

Later Pedro and I would laugh about this swift trick on my part. A natty head in a wicked situation, is a virtue where I come from.

"My wayward son, the bold Pedro, a credit to his teachers and land, but in need of a reprimand for his uppityness betimes," and so I led him away, my hand resting affectionately on both his shoulders.

"Thank you for getting me away from that mob," were his first words to me, his loving dad.

"If my nephew were half like you, I would be as proud as punch," I said.

"You are a strange and crazy fellow, that is why I like you," said Pedro.

"It is always better to subdue a threatening person before attempting to parley with him," I explained to him as he soothed his sores and bruises.

"That is something I do not immediately accept at its face value. Even though force is, to an extent a part of life, we distinguish between natural and unnatural uses of force. Eating food is a form of force and violence, but it is for a natural purpose, so is defensive hitting-back; but the kind of force you indulged in a while ago is very unnatural. Do you understand?"

He spoke very rapidly and professionally. I was impressed.

"Who taught you all that? You sure have a good memory."

"It is part of my philosophy. I am a runaway heretic from the Basque province in Espana, or Spain to you."

I can put you up in my place and even give you work there. It won't be what you might be used to, I'm sure, seeing as how lily-white your hands are, but it will enable you to earn a decent living."

"I thank you. Begging has been my source of sustenance for these last three years. A noble way of life but very tedious."

"And all because you are a man of truth. Well, that is the way the world is."

"Such charity can only come from a fellow-spirit. Perhaps I will be able to repay you some time."

Two is always safer company than one and I was beginning to feel uneasy in my isolation and new occupation in that strange city. Pedro was good company, his voice being very musical so that while he talked I was able to drift into a dream world and think my own thoughts and form my own conclusions.

He was a very helpful and co-operative companion. It was dark as we doubled back along the river. Just to put Pedro at his ease and to end his terrible scruples, I proceeded to present him with what in his own words, was "the greatest crisis of my life".

A lone man, hobbling on a stick and muttering to himself was lifted off the ground by me, tapped on the head and deposited in the river for all time.

"He was old and in pain and he won't be missed by anyone. Also he was very irritating with his mumbling."

Poor Pedro was speechless.

It was Pedro who first mentioned Amerigo Vespucci. He said that there was a fellow he knew, a Florentine, who had helped him to find a roof for his head in Cadiz, in the south of Spain. They became close friends and Pedro helped Amerigo in his studies. The Florentine was a clerk in his early days, but he had grown restless and departed for Spain with the intention of joining the Spanish Foreign Legion of the Seas. I forget what the Spanish title of that was.

Amerigo Vespucci discovered America. Pedro and myself were with him when he did. That is how it came to have the name of Amerigo. The second name of the place is Fadaland, I suppose it could be translated as. In case people there object that there was only one discoverer of the New World and that his name was Christopher Columbus, let me say that it is a false claim and that if people knew the real character of the immortal Columbus, he would not be so high in everybody's esteem. I can re-affirm that Amerigo and the rest of us left Cadiz on the tenth day of May in the year of fourteen ninety one, which was a year before Columbus got round to it. We landed on the mainland of America forty-four days later on June the sixteenth of that year. The actual place was on the northeast tip of South America. Anyway, I am jumping the gun here. Amerigo's name came up in the course of a discussion one evening on the subject of travelling. Amerigo, said Pedro, claimed that if he had the money, he would be able to organise an expedition to a new land that was filled with gold and good things and the first lucky one there would be made the emperor of the place. He said that Spain was the best country to start out from, but there was not much time, as others were in the race also.

There was a dispute going on between Vespucci and Columbus in which Columbus maintained that the earth was flat and that America did not exist, whereas Amerigo, against much ridicule (for the great majority supported Columbus), insisted on the roundness of the world and said that a new continent did exist.

"When I had to leave, the poor man was in tears. The loss of a friend was made more unbearable by the collapse of his plans. The police drove me out of town and his friendship with me was more than sufficient for him to lose all credit in the eyes of any potential sponsor. It is a sad story."

"Sure enough it is. He sounds very much like a gentleman to me. Anyone who is hounded by the people of his town is a man of truth. Perhaps one day you and I will go to Cadiz and look up this Amerigo."

I told Pedro then about the gold I had.

He worked hard giving out drinks while I held at bay all the mysterious customers and foreigners who crowded at the door and tried to break down the place. Attempts were made to knife me. Wealthy and important individuals would pop in and try to make all sorts of lucrative bargains with me. But I did not want to have anything to do with any of them, only wanting to run a respectable drinking place while I worked on my plans. After a time, I only allowed in a known and trusted clientele, so rowdy and troublesome had the majority of people become.

Pedro and I worked on schemes for me to become rich and famous quickly. Eventually, it was decided between the two of us that I would demonstrate the "Lame", an act known only to myself. This would become famous; we would earn large sums of money and thus be in a position to further spread my fame and increase my fortune and influence.

It is my own private opinion that Pedro was a little bit of a trick-artist. He was more of an artist than he himself realised. He considered himself to be a very serious and advanced philosopher, but sometimes I think he was something of a playboy. He was fond of getting innocent people into disputes with him on all sorts of subjects and then he would confuse them and somehow manage to get them feeling guilty about themselves and their lives and everything they ever did. Oftentimes I have seen poor harmless people leave weeping bitterly after talking with Pedro. The great philosopher was always going on about the persecution and the hard times he had to put up with in the service of what he called the truth but it looked to me as if he was making a profession of his numerous sufferings.

The importance of the deliberations of his thinking cannot be denied however and he wrote one book which was later done out in the newly-discovered print-form. He says that there is still a copy extant today. I read his own manuscript and there is one passage which I have never forgotten. The title of the book was "The Real Meaning of Death". I will quote from it the bit that I remember:

"It is a subject fascinating to us all – I constantly seek the answer. But Rome was not built in a day or the Bible written in a year. Death has now become familiar to each and everyone of us, especially in this day and age. Let us not dread it. My acquaintances have shown me that it is a very easy thing to bring about. There is absolutely no life after death. No one has returned to life to inform us of the existence of another world. The ending of our life has become the ground on which thinkers deliberate and theologians argue. They are all mad. What is death? It is the cessation of life. Surely that is as clear and as emphatic as daylight? Where is the problem? All will come to an end. It is the decay of life. That is the real meaning of death. It is the end of everything...."

Pedro was my adviser at the time and he set me thinking on many new problems of life. However the longer we live, and it cannot be denied that I have lived a long time, the greater is our wish to take only some of the advice that is offered to us, and to discard the rest. This is so regardless of the esteem in which we hold our adviser, or his attainments.

It would be a little boring to dwell too long once again on the subject of my personality and how it was developing and the changes that had newly become evident to me in my attitudes and feelings towards the world. Let it be suffice for me to say that these changes were dramatic, radical and never-ceasing. Some people thought me a strange man and I think they were a bit afraid of me as well. This was so despite my being extremely quiet in my words.

A growing intellectual awareness was mine under the careful tutelage of Pedro. An immense curiosity about new and unknown lands that awaited discovery, came to me. I developed opinions on all sorts of subjects that I never before knew existed. These opinions of mine became as strong and as unbreakable as those of any emperor. I learned as much as I could about Julius Caesar and Alexander the Great. I studied their characters and I made their traits mine. To Pedro, I gave as much honour and credit as he deserved. He was trustworthy and an adversary to all my enemies who were growing more numerous and determined every day. His advice proved to be wise on many occasions. I had to fight many pitched battles at the very gates of my domain. Needless to say, they were repulsed. It was not every man – not even the French king and princes – who could feel proud of having a learned man like Pedro by their side. I think their jealousy for me was great and they were not able to understand how it was that a man like Fada and a man like Pedro could become such good friends.

My dress was designed with much thought and consideration. I would call my tailor and tell him what particular virtues and attributes I had in mind and he would rush off to fulfill his task with loyalty and pleasure. I wore long flowing robes with the designs and images of the Gaelic chiefs of home. These were unintelligible to the French and so further increased my power. Although I kept my feet bare, except on certain occasions (shoes are an encumbrance to me and a cause of much distress), my head was always crowned with the biggest and grandest hat Paris had ever seen.

Pedro had by this time taken a wife and he would agree with me when I accused him of having become more fond of the comforts of life and neglectful of his more important duties. This woman was a smart wench. She was as slim as an eel and had a pointed head that turned swiftly whenever there was anything to see. It always appeared to be moving and I felt very uncomfortable in her presence. I believed that she was able to see things that men are not able to see. Her garb was smart and her tongue equally so. I knew that she didn't like me, because of my being a friend of her husband. There was still no doubt that it would be my bidding and not her's, that would be done by him in the last analysis.

Pedro expressed a feeling of satisfaction during the first few weeks of his marriage and then he became his normal self again and recommenced discussing the old subjects as if no change at all had taken place in his life.

So there you have the two of us, adventurous but wise souls, about to embark on a plan to bring us to the New World.

# Chapter Five

Much of Paris at this time was situated on a small island in the middle of the River Seine. It is where the famous Notre Dame is today, just over from the notorious Left Bank. The people were a queer mixture; some being the descendants of peasants who fled their cruel masters in the provinces; others, refugees from foreign lands, like myself. But we got on together not too badly, all being said and done. True, we had our quarrel and fisticuffs, but eventually even these became a part of accepted life and culture and were, in their own way, enjoyable.

It was into this scene that I introduced the "Lame".

Or rather, Pedro and I introduced The Act.

It was with mounting excitement that the citizens of the fair city saw posters go up all round advertising the act. It was to be introduced with a performance by the bold Pedro, philosopher extraordinary.

Then there would be an interlude of music, to be followed by the gala unveiling of the "lame", whose nature would not be revealed until opening night. Paris had not seen anything like it for ages. Preparations went in hand speedily."

At this stage Fada's voice disappeared suddenly and completely. Those sitting around looked at me with puzzlement and a little anxiety in their faces.

"It is allright. Everything is under control," I said.

But that was far from the truth and I did not know what had happened. Then a new and strange voice came over, loud and clear. It was almost as if the speaker were breathing down our necks, so overpowering was it.

One or two of the guests put their hands to their ears, and I was really sorry now they ever came.

"The possibilities of multiple personality spoil the resort to the Cogito as an irrefragable certitude. In a novel I won't name but which I was once accused of plagiarising, the 'I' of the story is told by the automatic writing of his own hand that he is only a secondary personality produced by stress; which suggests the doubt 'perhaps I am not a substantive person, but only a pathological condition' – a rather worse suspicion than that one is only a thing in somebody's dream. Unlike Descartes's demon, the conditions that would give rise to such doubt do actually exist. In view of all this, we cannot regard the Cogito as giving us a ready access to an identifiable immaterial somewhat that might conceivably survive transference from one body to another. Even if ambition or some other vice or virtue were infectious, one that I caught from him could hardly be regarded as an individual entity which persisted through the transference from him to me, like a microbe physically transferred. If the preceding arguments are sound, my present self-consciousness cannot avail to give me an understanding of such propositions as 'I lived before the Christian era', 'I decided to cross the Rubicon', etc."

There is no need to tell you that Pedro was on the line.

"If ever there was a danger of me losing the confidence of my friends and patrons in the room, it was now. For I could see that of all that Pedro had said to date, not a word of it was understood by anybody. Something had to be done."

At the top of my voice:

"Hold it Mr Pedro, some other time if you please. These people here have come a long distance and at great personal cost to hear your friend, Fada: they are anxious that the good man be allowed to finish his tale. I am sure you will understand what I am talking about."

"Well – if that is the way it is to be. If a little bit of philosphy from an unknown book is too much for you – when it was the very food of the ancients – then you cannot say much for the present generation. What do you think about at all? Tell me that. I suppose it is that new-fangled wireless and television that is the cause of it. We are well aware of these things up here you know – don't think that because we have been dead these past few centuries we are to be written off. We are not. And we still have feelings believe it or not. I would not expect the present modern-day generation to understand anything. Nobody understood me when I was alive so I would be foolish to expect them to do so now I am dead. So if you want to hear boring old Fada you can. He is just gone for a refreshment. But I can tell you a few interesting things too. And let me say also, in all solemnity, old Fada doesn't always tell the whole truth. I would even go as far as to say that he has told you a few untruths already, but he doesn't know I have been listening. Sh, sh. Here he comes. Don't tell him I've been talking to you."

★ ★ ★

Oho me boys. There is no telling you the excitement that was in Paris on the day of our first performance. The little children were running everywhere, spreading the word of what was about to take place and crying, ''Come see Fada's show ... nobody but Fada himself knows what it is... .''

The women that day were singing little tunes to themselves, happy at the thought of an evening away from drudgery and grateful to Fada for providing them with this liberation. Happy they were too perhaps, at the chance to see the man Fada himself, whose name and fame were already on the lips of many. They were humming and singing when they got up that morning, and they were humming and singing as they went about the preliminary tasks of the day, and they were humming and singing as they prepared to leave the house for the show; and as they came up many routeways to the place of the great event, they hummed and they sang.

The menfolk of that mighty city only worked for half a day, the rest of the afternoon being spent in drinking and chatting and preparing for the show. Ah, the whole of Paris was coming. They would come not once, but every evening and by the end of the week we would have enough money not only for a visit to the New World, but a visit to Heaven also.

A huge tent had been made ready and refreshments were there for those who wanted them. By six o'clock the tent was full of people and loud was the hum of their expectant voices. A band was playing music, which was of a kind that perhaps would not be familiar to you now, as neither would be the instruments they played. I have not seen their kind anywhere else. High indeed did the early moon rise in the sky in the paleness of its own watching face. Pedro came on at half-past six, by which time I had collected a fortune in cash. Some gold, silver, bronze, fine objects of art, books, drawings, trinkets, silks, livestock were all collected in payment. It was a better quality of money than exists today, let me say.

The queue went back one thousand seven hundred and sixty yards, a line of gentlefolk, rough folk, rich and poor folk, of noble folk. Some were quiet and afraid, some were loud – laughing and talkative. With the appearance of Pedro on stage there was a stunned silence. For, would you believe it, the chap had nothing on. Well, that was a surprise, to one and all, each and everybody, ladies and clergymen, lords and merchants, native and foreign. He sat on a chair. Then he looked at the audience and said;

"Good folk, good evening and welcome to the show. This will consist in two parts, the first which will be me and the second, the highlight of the whole thing, Fada the man himself. I am a philosopher and my contribution will be a bit of philosophising. As you might realise, it is a great pleasure for me to be in your lovely country where I believe, anything goes. To be able to undress – sorry, address – in front of you tonight is for me, a great double pleasure. Last month I got married. This has increased my urge for philosophy and that is a third reason I am honoured to appear before you like this, this evening."

By now, the crowd were with him and loud applause broke out all over the theatre, loud clapping and the canvas flapping outside in the wind, making an exciting sound. My heart was glowing.

"Each show this week will bring a different subject to be discussed. Tonight, we are looking at the proposition that History is bunk. Who said that? Who was the person who first made such a controversial statement? As soon as we know who it was, we will examine his character and see if he was a truthful and honest person. So, I ask you, who made that statement? Hands up if you know."

Various hands reluctantly appeared around the big top. When requested, each volunteered a name. Nobody could guess the right answer. After a while of this, Pedro shouted:

"Stop, stop. Folks, you are going to be very surprised when you hear the correct answer. What would you say, dear folk, if I told you it was me?"

Loud laughter ripped through the tent. My heart was pleased for Pedro was really getting them into the spirit of things.

At this stage it was quietly reported to me that certain individuals were trying to get in without paying, by climbing up the canvas. I had arranged for any such likelihood to be reported to me immediately, so that all action would be my own monopoly. I had not yet lost my willpower, or my strength, in all my time abroad, in a soft city like Paris. Out with me in a flash. A hefty helper took my place at the door.

"Be back in a jiffy," I said with joyful confidence.

"Have you ever climbed a high canvas tent after somebody, at high speed? No, I suppose not. It is great fun, especially when you have in store the further pleasure of flinging criminals all the way down again. Inside Pedro was going on with his act and their laughs were loud. Apparently, I heard later, a lot of the laughter was caused by the ructions up on the canvas of me and them, which had a little disturbed the show below. The gutter-snipes could not get away from me and I nabbed the three of them easily. They squealed and snarled like the rats they were, and then pleaded with me for to give them a chance, as they put it.

"I'll give you a chance, all right," I said grimly between my teeth.

"The chance I have in store for you is the chance that you'll either break your neck, or not break your neck but your legs."

They cried and squealed all the more.

"My two broad arms encircled their scraggy necks. My roar of glee shook them all the more and indeed, shook the tent. At the top there was a big hole and I could see inside and Pedro's tiny head. My shout like a wind went down to them.

"Hey Pedro. Look up here."

They all looked up.

"What will I do with these three cheats? What do you say?"

A murmur I heard go through the crowd. There followed moments of confusion and mighty sounds. Then with a wave of his hands Pedro silenced the multitude. He spoke gravely.

"What the hell is going on? This is an unsatisfactory opening. There is an interruption into my show that is very unexpected indeed. There is somebody up above us."

"It is Fada," I shouted down.

"Looking up at me was the placid face of Pedro. Also, at one staring upwards, was the audience. A pretty sight. You may be sure the crowd were asking each other what was going to happen here. Perhaps with trepidation also. Aha me boyos, it was my time. Their cries only increased my joy."

"I have three quare ones here. Thieves of the worst kind they are. What should be done with them, Pedro?", was my enquiry.

Calm and silence descended over the town of Paris. Inside and outside the tent was the whole population, waiting. The mass of folks was like a swarm of bees. Pedro had everything well under control.

"Dear folks, kings, nobles, ladies and gentlemen. We are presented with a problem by the bold Fada. The matter that must be judged is whether it is more worthwhile to drop the criminal element down so that they will smash their bones in front of us or, in the other case, with a pat on the back and a whisper of kind truth in their ears, to return them swiftly to their mothers. I hope you all recognise the moral issue when you see it, for on your judgment depends the lives of some fellow-human beings."

"The grunts and coughs that followed a period of doubting silence signalled that the people had come to a decision. A strange, serious-looking clerk of an individual stood up and waved a pale hand at the nervous, giggling faces. He asked that those in favour of dropping them say 'aye' and those against 'nay'. In direct translation that would be 'oui' and 'non'. Well. It was a laugh. Didn't half of them say 'oui' and the other half 'non'? The referee was confused and turned around for advice. This is what transpired.

"Fada, up there," said Pedro, "You have the casting vote."

"Well, here it is," I cried, and cast them down to their doom. They were carried off the stage. I made my way down the tent to find the philosopher concluding stage one of the proceedings with a loud and intense harangue of the crowd, who appeared mystified by the whole thing. Little could I blame them for what he was doing now was beyond my immediate grasp. At last he stopped and retired backside to the front. I wondered the effect this was having on my reputation. A funny looking Combo trotted up on stage now to the laughter of the happy audience. They (the musicians) were constantly twittering and running about and soon set up a rhythm that only seemed to suit their twittering. I determined to speak pronto to the one whose responsibility it was for getting that Combo. Soon it would be time for my act, the show's high point and what was keeping everybody in trepidation. A trumpeter had been obtained for "Le Grand Entrance", when I would come out from my dressing room behind the stage. It was there I retired to and put on my stage clothes in all their gaiety. To give myself an aura of great importance, I had a retinue of many people in waiting on me. They all showed the greatest respect to me, bowing down and waving their arms about and so on. Heavy boots were put on my feet. They were made of leather and were much better than the rubber articles around these days, excuses for boots. I decided that for the occasion, heavy clothing would be the most apt, gaily decorated with colourful designs. Crisp orders I delivered right, left and centre the better to increase my image of professionalism, for these Paris people only admire things that are well done. At last, let us not delay the moment, everything was ready for a historic act that had never been seen done before and has never been done since I walked the earth. The "Lame". Or the "Jump". Great applause broke out as our entourage entered onto the stage. At the back there were a few boos, to be expected in any circumstances, but there were plenty of people to take care of anyone who seriously attempted to disturb the show or make a nuisance of themselves. You can imagine the set-up. What the hell of a racket they were making all right. What would happen if the show proved to their dissatisfaction? That is a question the answer to which filled me with dread.

A chair was put out for my sitting while Pedro went on with a whole rigmarole about my past, the history (to date) of Eire, the multivarious adventures that brought me to the 'Heaven On Earth', their very own and world famous city, gay Paris. Loud trumpet calls punctuated at intervals what he was saying. At every mention of my name, there was a mandatory pause of five seconds and a triple trumpet call. You can imagine that the more impressionable members of the audience were in an intense state of excitement by now.

When silence came on them, I took over. A slow, low rendition of an old popular tune, "We bring the summer with us," I gave to their satisfaction. A long, rambling tale of the two drunken rabbits I gave to their amusement. A story of sadness concerning the runaway jackasses I gave to their sorrow. The jigsaw about the case of the old woman and the missing bowl of porridge I gave to their puzzlement. About the man who walked three hands above the surface the woods, bogs and seaways was to their awe. About the game of chess overwhelmed them. At last I introduced the main attraction. I explained simply that it had never been seen in public before and that I was the only person in the world who was capable of performing it. That it was the most amazing thing in the world would soon be seen. That its fame would live for ever was accepted even by Pedro, who knew all things. A few jeers and objections came to my ears but there are always those kind of people about and my men were taking note of them and preparing punishment.

"THE LAME" I shouted suddenly and every eye was staring.

A slow uplift came to my person and I arose out of my seat. My expression as natural as if I were still seated, every eye watched my progress upwards in unbelief. I reached the roof without the aid of lines, wires or pulleys. No strings. At the top I casually waved my arms to the side to show that it had been done naturally. Just as casually and quite slowly I let myself down again.

"It is all physical strength, pure and simple," I said.

Some people had actually fainted at the spectacle, believing, I suppose, that the aid of the devil had been enlisted. A loud and steady applause filled the tent, the likes of which sounded as thunder and storm on the sea. To what cause can be attributed the delirium that accompanied their reception of the Lame? In what realm of understanding can be explained the rapturous fame that was attached to my name thereafter? Why should such a performance, such a pure and simple feat of physical exertion, well-known to the wild Kerry men and not much commented on there, a standard act at all the ancient Gaelic fairs, be such a big hit in the capital of the world's art? The Paris people received it as their own and promptly accorded it a Parisian name, a French title which I cannot remember as I did not bother to translate it. I thought it was cheek though.

The King of Paris himself came up on stage to compliment me and he asked me, by the way, was it a trick and did they use it in Ireland to help themselves in battle, and if so, could I teach it to his own troops and he would be very grateful and would reward me well. I was inwardly and secretly pleased that that particular gentleman had been impressed, for it was important to be on the good side of kings and nobility in those days (is it not still true today?), if one had ambitions.

To what best use could I put my act, to be assured of raking in as much money as possible from it here in Paris, that was my question. I said I would like an official audience with his Majesty, in private sometime, and he agreed with a nod of his head, thereby almost losing his crown.

The Lame was put on every day for the next seven days and all Paris and many from the provinces came as gaping guests. Pedro and I were quite well-off by the end of it and other diverse persons in that city, people whose livelihood was earned by carrying on all manner of shady tricks, show-people they called themselves, complained about us and cast aspersions on our act, just because it outshone anything they ever did or were ever likely to do. Not to mention the fact that we were quite successfully taking away from their own business. Anyway, to sum things up, I was a wealthy enough man by now, although I missed the old sod a bit and still found foreign parts strange. There was also the gift of gold, to add to my wealth. This I always kept well-hidden and its presence I hoped, was known to no one in Paris, having well-learnt my lesson about the greed of mankind from the nephew. In those days, gold was scarce, them having not yet discovered it in the New World. If anyone guessed that in my possession there was a bag of this substantial metal, I do not think my life could have held out against the hordes of nifty thieves that would surely immediately descend on my harmless presence. And, believe me, included in the horde would also be, diverse bishops, befrocked of Holy days, well-known friends, kings, nobles and women. Not to mention the rat-bag denizens of the sewers. Who would protect me then? In my bed-living room at the time was a timbered trestle that was my place of rest. On a wooden plank, bare of anything, each night was my sleeping abode. It was this that was my tradition from my days of youth, while in this place there lay an additional advantage in that such a posture involved a sleep lighter than would be normal in a softer bed, thus ensuring a quick awakening in the event of an unwanted invasion. Eye-quick indeed was my sleep, as it still is to this day. As I am at it, let me describe to you the accidentals of the rest of my room, as it would have looked at daytime. My marvellous attire was carefully hung up in various places, each in its colour set apart from the next and each treated equally in respect. The chiefs of the New World, of Amerigo's land, have been known to wear feathers as tall as the trees and as colourful as the rainbow and everyone of equal and increasing importance as the next. In a similar fashion there was in my own possession a garment for every occasion and a hat for every performance. My most important hat was a plumed affair, as tall as myself again, and every bit as good-looking as a king's crown. Where did I hide the gold, you might be wondering? That is a matter I always kept to myself under any and every circumstance, there being no reason to change such a rule now.

Bread and wine with a smattering of salt before and after meals was my chief diet. Although thick and blood-red beef was always my favourite food, all the time I was in Paris I did not partake of animal's flesh, following the advice and example of Pedro who informed me that a typical Parisian trick was to gorge outsiders with rich food and entertainment and then when they are too full and satisfied, content and sleepy, to grab them unawares and make mincemeat of them. Vegetables were better, he said. Although also the pronounced occupation of Pedro, his habitual talent, was claimed to be philosophy, the metaphysical science of seeing into the future, it was one in which my confidence had slipped; nevertheless I still valued his practical advice which, strange though it often sounded, had a way of coming true, perhaps due to his philosophical training.

And it was so that there was a scarcity of time available in my heavy schedule for the finer pursuits of light pleasures or fun. As much as I or any man is fond of the titillation of the senses, it is always wise to afford them second place to the completion of business. Suffice that my early-morning run around the outskirts of the city granted a pleasurable release of the senses, a clearing of the lungs and a stressing of the muscles.

What did Pedro do with himself, you might wonder? Well, he spent less and less time with the wife, much to my approval. He took to long walks in quiet places when he was not involved in business matters with me. He expressed now and again an unsettled feeling, an itchy foot, a desire to go somewhere where he had never been before. Little did he, or I, know how completely that wish was to be fulfilled. Pedro also sought out strange heretics and famous gurus, in hidden confines of the town, to debate with them. Presuming he was thinking on the usual existential problems, little did I guess the real train of thought that was coursing through his tiny brain at the time.''

"Wake up, wake up," I had to tell the dozing listeners, "how can you be so slighting of Fada's true tale, when he has come back from the dead and is expending so much energy in the telling? Do not fall into slumber, for I feel that the most interesting piece is to come.''

"An earthquake shook Paris that weekend and caused multiple deaths and many buildings to fall. Deep cracks appeared in the earth... .''

At this point, the whole room began to shake and the walls appeared to topple. My poor folks were alarmed and shouted as their chairs moved. A warning to them by me to hold steady, that it would pass, was faithfully obeyed by one and all. A thunderous roar from within the ground was like a lion and all Hell seemed to have come loose. They were clinging on to one another as the sounds of Paris trembling filled the room. Glasses on the table toppled and I do not believe any of them had much hope of escape. Then the voice of Fada returned from above the thunder. I could see that they were terrified out of their wits and relief appeared on their faces when the now familiar voice was heard once more.

"Pedro and I were walking along a busy back-street when it struck. It was a Monday and our run of shows were all over and we were pondering together what to do next. The earthquake helped us to make up our minds for, as Pedro said, it was not a good thing and more were likely to follow. The houses in the street fell down, missing us each time but hitting many other people. The worst thing that happened was me getting temporarily stuck in a deep crevice but I easily hauled myself out. We said that we should visit His Majesty before we left, to be of mutual assistance. Long may he reign, and his children after him.''

"At this point, Fada's voice changed and he spoke more slowly, in an explanatory way.''

"Do not worry if you felt the effects of the earthquake as I spoke, for it is my wish that you all get the best picture you can of life in the old days and experience as much as possible the sweet things and the terrible things that I went through and that changed me so completely at the end, as you shall see.''

# Chapter Six

"The king, someone told us, had a hut somewhere, but this was only the entrance to his palace, which was invisible from the highway. We, the two of us, Pedro and I, set out for to enquire about the way to this hut, which we believed was an ordinary gate-lodge. It was a queer state of affairs that honest citizens we met and asked along the way ignored us or even if they did speak, refused to tell us the whereabouts of this gate-lodge. Another queer thing was that neither Pedro or myself had any clue as to where this Royal fellow was king of. The gentleman with whom we were wishing to do some business-talking might have been a king only in his own imagination, we were thinking at the end of it. At the heel of the hunt, down by a meadow near the river where the two of us were admiring some young ladies, a cheeky rascal came up and said, in a gutter Paris voice:

"Monsieurs. It is a fine time of day for the sport of gentlemen. For the sum of a small figure, I am at your service, sirs. Please look upon me as a servant."

He was a cringing type, who reminded me of the nephew. I presume you all remember him and are not nodding off, bad luck though it is to hear even the mention of his name. We asked this young man the way to the king's house, but we had to give a complete description of the monarch first, as, we were informed, that there were dozens of kings and princes around. As far as Pedro and I could remember, the fellow who came to speak to us at the Great Tent was very tall with a heavy crown which looked very awkward on the poor man. He had freckles on his face and an everlasting glow in his eyes. Our newly acquired friend, if you could call him that, said that this was the famous king Thuk who had terrorised his subjects for decades of years. His palace was behind old trees and we had to go through the gate-lodge first. The old trees, as he described them, were a straight two French miles up the river.

"Follow the bank," he said.

I left it to Pedro to reward the gentleman fairly with our gold and our silver and when I heard the grunt and looked back to see Pedro withdrawing the sharp knife from the man, I knew that the just desserts had been given. When we came to the gate-lodge hut, believe it or not, we were afraid to go in. Neither the "bold" Pedro nor your's truly would make the first move. Fine heroes, I tell you. A fine pair. Eventually, for it is hard to persuade a philosopher, I went in myself to be pleasantly surprised both by the warmth of the greeting I received and by one of the personages who was giving the greeting, for it was the very same king himself. To raise up his esteem, I fell to the ground and kissed it in front of him, the better too, to put him at his ease. He laughed and said he was delighted to see me and that he had been expecting me and the fact that I had come showed how right he was to have been expecting me. The comforts of the house were at my disposal and that if any man, woman or child should happen to chance cross me in the wrong way, he would see to it. After a while, Pedro's head appeared at the door and I shouted, laughing at the same time that it was safe for him and all his dear ones to enter in and no harm would befall them.

"Have you brought your magic cloth?", the old king said, me not having a clue what in hell he was speaking of.

"No," I said, "I think I left it behind. What magic cloth?"

"That which lifts you to the Heavens. The old and venerable powers of the East. You know what I mean?"

He grinned at me and for once, I did not like it. He took us out to a field after a drink of wine and put his royal hand on my back, for it did not reach to my shoulder. He said that in a minute his "men" would come by and that I would be exalted by the sight of them. In the meantime we sat on a fence and talked about various things. Large animals galloped around in the far distance and the sun broke out overhead. Winds sang tunes in our ears and the whole world had taken on to itself a French nature, for me. Pedro used to laugh whenever I spoke of things French. It was all a mockery for him. It was also a fact at the same time that he did not admire anything that came from Spain, the dear land of his birth but not death. So it was not any misguided patriotism that led Pedro into loud snuffles at the mention of the grand things of France. The funny side of this business now was that when I said to his Royal Highness that France looked very beautiful today Pedro stayed quiet and did not laugh or anything. It did not raise him in my view when I pondered that it was fear or awe in the presence of an idiot chief – a petty one at that – that kept Pedro in his place.

"Here they come," said his majesty. And with a grand wave of his arm the lot of them appeared over the rise. And a right rise they gave to me too; fearful and amazing were they, leading me to make a similar comment to the king as that made by a general at a famous battle centuries later.

"They are my best troops and I would send them anywhere," he had said proudly, "as long as I do not have to accompany them."

"Long live France," he shouted at them when they came to a halt.

"Ole," they shouted back, or at least it was something sounding like that; what French soldiers would be doing speaking Spanish I don't know. I counted them, there were ten. The king explained that these were the generals; the men were out defending a place. He asked us to teach the Top Brass our skills.

"Which one, or all of them?", was my query, as much bidding for time as anything else.

"Come on," he said, poking me in the ribs; "teach them how to rise to the sky. Undefeatable in battle will they be then, thanks to you."

Pedro called me aside and whispered in my ear that the king would try to conquer the whole world if we were to impart "The Lame" – that old Ireland would not be exempt from his tyranny and that no person could be ever free thereafter.

"We were just talking about tactics," I explained to His Lordship when we had finished.

"Your reward will be beyond your expectations," he promised us.

Once again Pedro pulled me aside with an astounding look of fear in his face and I was becoming a bit annoyed with him. He explained his worry.

"Do you think I was born yesterday?", I asked; "I have already thought a way out of the danger while you were still wetting yourself. What kind of philosopher are you anyway?"

I gave the king a beautiful smile and suggested we get started. Into the middle of the grass we all went and I told the soldiers to line up in a line. So that we would quickly become chums I called them "sirs" and lifted my hat to them in honouring fashion. At the same time with a sad grin and friendly wink I pointed my head in the direction of his majesty and returned it in an instant to give a knowing look to the onlooking men. Did they get my message, that was a question that I would be unable to answer for some moments of time?

For it was my wish to take from the poor king his army. An evil thought indeed, and hanged be all accursed thieves, but it was my only aim to save the world. Greed was not in my heart. Judge for yourselves, friends, if not what I say is the truth, for great though may have been the developments in my character since I had left the Holy Land, and great though have always been the mystery of my life to me, my childhood mother-taught honesty never has left my side, as she is my Judge and ye all too, soon.

"Your highness," I said, "before I teach them the most marvellous feat known to man and wondered at in the Heavens even, before I bestow on your army the power envied in the Underworld, it is wise that they go for a little jog to sharpen their elbows and brighten their minds. With Pedro at their head and I, Fada, at their rear; they will be looked over with wisdom. Is that all right, your majesty?"

"Do as you will, my friends. Your wisdom is undoubted."

The blackguard! The bostun! There he was, thinking he had got us by the neck. My blood boiled. The generals got in a heap and before we set off I asked them where this battle was that their soldiers were partaking in and would it be possible there and then to go and collect them. Their reply was not in the negative.

"Soon be back," was my assurance to the King of the World standing behind me.

With that, lo and behold, we were off like jackrabbits out of a trap and away with us over the brow of the hill. That was the last we ever saw of the king. I have seldom, in a life long and not unmixed, met a chancer of the last resort, a greater hoaxer and conman, one whose claims to greatness were as exaggerated as his strength was mean, as that so-called king of God-Knows-Where. I wonder what became of him, or where he is now?

Did you ever see a great big balloon go up in the air and sail gracefully like for hundreds of miles? All colourful and gay? That is the manner of our progression from Paris into deeper lands uncharted after that. As blessed we were as the daisies of heaven and surely we were looked upon with favour. So spirited did we feel that later, when I suddenly remembered that Pedro had a wife, and I mentioned it to him in surprise, so greater still was his own surprise. For a long time after that the little man carried on long conversations with himself, why he had left her and whether it was right or wrong. In the end, I think I persuaded him that there was no such thing as right or wrong, for it was right that the wrong of stealing my cattle be done, as now I was enjoying life instead of being stuck in a field; that it was wrong that the right be done of taking the evil king's army away from him, for thievery is thievery – that such was the progression of my thoughts that I let my heart rule my head and that my heart knew no feeling, but was now as cold as a stone. For long hours I held forth on these and other subjects with Pedro, and with the three hundred soldiers – for we had picked up more armies along the way – gathered in the heat of the firelight.

The crackling flames were a great joy in which to warm ourselves in the cold hours the night, and the men seemed more than happy in the new leadership of Fada by the glow on their faces. "In all events Pedro," I said, "you did not leave her but forgot her."

"I wish I could believe so, but the mind is a funny thing," said the poor fellow.

As we marched through the countryside with scarcely a care in the world, a new feeling of pride came into me, such as the possession of a thousand cows could not equal. Along the way there came up to join with us many individuals. Our numbers grew and our fame went before us. It was reported to me that people were awaiting our arrival all over the land. In the towns and villages preparations were being made for weeks before we came; and on our entry into these places, we were greeted by garlands and the ring of their loud cries in our ears.

"Look at these people, Pedro," I said, "do you know why they call out in such emotion? It is because they are looking for someone to deliver them out of their hardships, which I presume are many. Their pinched faces show hunger and drudgery is their way of life. The fame of Fada at fun and at fight has gone before us and it has caused great wonder and great fear. I have decided to deliver them from their mortal chains and to take to myself their own goods."

Pedro took it into his head to start a discussion of the matter and I hit him so hard that he ended up high in a nearby tree. The fright that this put on the faces of the soldiers was immense, but the anger that was in my own eyes was even greater.

"Come down from that tree measily philosopher and help us rob the folk and then to proceed to Rome to see what is there and also to give the greetings of a dear one to the Pope."

That great were the inflictions we proceeded to inflict on terrified country folk at that place and at others, cannot be denied. But there was mercy too, on my part, and I often spared the old women and young children.

As for the soldiers of Fada, there was little trouble from them and they showed much loyalty to me. I forbade them to have any rapport with women along the way and this was a rule which was to be strictly enforced. That land was surely strange that we travelled through. At first it caused wonder and uneasiness in me, such as I had when I first arrived in this place I am in up here. As well as the strangeness of the countryside, there was the wickedness of the many traps that were set in our way so that there was tedium and effort in our having to devise new tricks for survival. Any Irishman knows what it is like to have to walk through a bog in the middle of the night; well we had to travel often in the dark hours and I can tell you that it was an even more difficult proposition. There were many harrowing hours when we didn't know what was under our feet. I don't think that greater trials have been offered to any leader, or greater dangers put in any man's way. There were many unusual things to be seen in that country; but the most unusual thing I have ever seen anywhere were the tombs. I have not figured out yet what they were. The land was strewn with tombs. At first I believed they were mountains but everyone of them had a door into it. The trees stood like wrestlers in our way and the plants were like strangling arms. Often we were to lose soldiers in these bushes, whose lost cries would come to our ears as we went on with our march.

Then we came into valleys of great beauty, whose pleasantness was like a dream and where the men were lulled asleep by the ease of living and the warmth of the blue mist. This caused them to pay less attention to my commands and my talk, to which they were most attentive when they had only the mossy roots of damp trees as their nourishment and there were no birds around to sing to them in their slumber. So I decided to avoid in the future the easy paths and scenic routes, and to stick like mountain-goats to the hard out-of-the-way places. Fearful of their enemies who pursued them at every turn, nothing was treated lightly by the men of the army of Fada. The night even, whose cloak gave us protection, was considered by some to be a foe and they wished to pierce its shining stars which were like spies to them. The moon shouted to them as would a bellowing harlot and at it they aimed their spears and arrows. We fell into deep holes in the ground and it was necessary to send some of our prisoners walking ahead of us, in order that we might know what we were coming to.

My impatience and my wonder at the strangeness of the places we passed through I did not show, and the dependence of my followers on me was as loyal as are the ticks on a horse's back. As the numbers of dangers that we faced increased, so too did the loudness of their support. Their faults and their unworthy deeds I constantly held before them; I reminded them of their own base nature; their sloth I showed them before their own eyes. I told them I was bringing them to a safe and a prosperous haven, where they could enjoy their ill-gotten gains, while not knowing in my own mind where I was even as I spoke. Such is the challenge of leadership. Many gave their lives willingly for me. Some went ahead in search of ambushers and never returned. Others, with great fury, attacked the giants, the monsters and the hard-walled houses that we met along the way, and lost their lives with no hesitation, at my bidding.

Nevertheless, I did not understand anything of what we were coming across. I had believed until then that the world was the same everywhere you went. I thought that it came to an end at the horizon and that our eyes could see all that was in the world. It was a puzzle and a mystery to me when new objects appeared and we came across sights that I had never seen before."

At this point in the proceedings, another silence fell on the voice. We waited. There was less surprise in us now, as we were becoming used to these interruptions. The guests appeared as if they were resigned now to hearing all that Fada had to say, despite their earlier trepidation. I wondered if there was a sneaking admiration at the back of their minds for me. They jumped when Pedro came on the line again.

"He is gone for a minute and this is a good opportunity for me to get in a word. It was me who gave advice and information to the big fellow in our trek across France. It was a wise partnership; that between the brawn of Fada and the brains of Pedro. I have been in existence for many centuries now and I have seen the chief events of history. I have looked down at the riots of the great revolutions; I have observed the destruction of cities and of whole ways of life, many of which I was not sad to see go. The public and the secret deaths of many kings have not escaped my eye. Indeed, on many occasions I have even gone down to be present at the activities of man, although of course I would have been invisible to anybody else there. I won't bore you with comments on the past follies of man, but how would you like a prophecy or two? I can do it for free."

I don't think the guests were so keen about this, for their faces were pale and Pedro must have brought back again their old feeling of insecurity.

"Man is always afraid of what he does not understand. He also has a great knack of hiding from the truth when it stares him in the face. One prophecy I give is that you will all die. How about that?"

I must say I did not like the way this Pedro was talking, as he had caused one poor person to start snivelling, and it all seemed so unnecessary. It was a hard enough job to get them settled down in the first place, without going out of one's way to cause trouble. I wondered where Fada was.

"A prophecy is a fact of life. I have always found it to be the case that human beings like to think it is they who have created the world. They like to think that they can change its laws as they wish. They are gods to themselves. Do you want to know the future of the world? Did you ever hear about the Roman emperor, the Spanish king, the Russian czar, the African chief, the Chinese mandarin and the Irish high king, and the bit of nonsense they got up to up here? But Fada is returning and I am skidooing. Enjoy yourselves."

★　★　★

"Wretches may come and wretches may go, but that one goes on for ever. What has he been up to? I am back after a drink. I said to Pedro, let's take a turn to the left and visit Rome, as I have promised someone a favour. The Pope resides there and he has much wealth. I hear he is a charitable man. Pedro had a fit and a half when he heard my announcement. As you know, he was a Free-thinker. He was scandalised."

"Excuse me for a minute, Fada," I said, "I want to say a few words to my friends here."

Fada obeyed immediately. I then made a private address to them, asking if they had noticed any change at all in the proceedings. One man said yes, he had; that they had come to an end. I don't know what he meant by that. I gave a hint – it was in Fada's voice and manner of speaking. No? Well, I told them with some amusement that he had become a bit tipsy and that he was sounding giddy. Listen carefully and you will notice it, I told them.

"Carry on Fada."

"What was I talking about? The Pope. I pretended to Pedro that the pope was my idol for I got enjoyment out of giving him a rise. As I reflected aloud on the satisfaction I felt at the prospect of a visit to Rome, he was squirming and putting on the face of a mad rat. No need to tell you it gave me the encouragement to go on all the more. I kept this kind of talk up for days. However, the bloody little squirt had some arguments of a practical nature against our plan for proceeding down that way; arguments which I pretended to ignore, but which secretly I turned over in my private thoughts. One of these was that, by cutting sideways across our previous track which had been going in a straight line downwards, we were, as the philosopher illustrated by means of a line drawn in the mud, asking for double trouble by exposing our army from everyside, whereas in the way we had been going, the army was subject to attack from just two directions. I had to agree in the quiet of my own mind that it was the case.

"Let us go to Spain instead. We can gather more gold and treasure in along the way and by the time we get there, we will have enough for a ship and more. The world is at our feet now, Fada; it would be foolish to put it all at risk just in order to pay a courtesy call on a Church dignitary."

It was a sensible and wise summing up of matters, which was one of the reasons why I rejected his conclusions and came to my own instead. For no leader can afford to show himself to be dependent on his advisers, and if he is to be a leader, he should stick to his own thoughts, whether they be right or wrong.

"I will go to see the Pope and ask his blessing for my aunt," I said to the assembled troops. Not one of them as much as grimaced.

We swept to the left and Pedro said that we were like locusts going over rice fields. We did not have any dilly-dalliers. If anyone was caught wasting time picking fruit or berries, or resting up in the trees, he was hung up by the toes on the spot and left there. Then we came to those very high mountains in that part of the world. Just before we started our climb of these, there was the affair of Dalia. Half-naked she was brought to me. I was told that she was found to be spying on the men. It was only much later and unfortunately much too late, that I came to believe that they were lying to me and that the poor girl was innocent after all. It happened like this. I was asleep in my carriage. This was a great big box which my men carried me in over long distances. It was my pride and joy in those days and I usually held my conferences while sitting inside it. In its shade I slept as everybody rested and did whatever they did in their spare time. She was carried to me screaming and bawling and scraping like a cat so the hair of her captors was torn out and their faces were bloody. I liked her immediately. The man told me this spying story and his friends agreed that it was the truth. She would not speak to me at first in the silence of my box. Fear had temporarily unbalanced her mind. Also I do not think that she understood the foreign words in which I spoke. As I watched her, a fever came into my body and a sickness overcame me. I wondered if she was a witch and if she had put a spell on me. I went to Pedro for advice. For once he was silent and he did not even attempt to offer an opinion. I thought it was very unusual, but I did not wish to give the appearance of being uncertain in my own mind, so I did not persist with my questions to him. The whole business still gives me pain, for Fada should never make a mistake. He decided that the safest course would be to have her killed. I cannot say much more on this subject, for I would prefer to forget it, if that was possible. Perhaps she was a spy after all. Maybe it was the only way to get rid of the spell which caused me discomfort in her presence, and which gave great confusion to my thoughts. Was she a witch and a spy? It is a question that can never be answered for certain. I am sorry I have brought the subject up. Excuse me."

"Off for another quick one," I joked to the audience.

"In the mountains of the Alps there are many convenient valleys given over for men to travel through. These passes had paved roads and numerous resting spots and drinking fountains. And it was these very passes that we avoided, keeping instead to the steep ways. Thus it was that we became very cold, but fast running and toil were sufficient to reduce the cold, and to give us some heat. Snow we used both as food and as drinking water, and snowballs we flung in order to keep in trim for battle. On one mountain, at my suggestion, a statue of snow, of immense features, was made in my likeness. I wonder is it still standing to this present day? Perhaps I will take a trip down there to the Alps one day and have a look.

I began to notice that Pedro had become very quiet and he would only come to my carriage when I called him. Then he was sullen and he didn't even try to make conversation. I put up with this for a while, thinking it was just a passing mood in his case. But he kept it up and in the end I lost patience with him.

"Pedro. What is the matter with you? Tell me what is on your mind and leave nothing out."

"Are you completely sure you wish me to take part in a frank discussion with you?", he replied strangely.

"So long as you address me with respect and on your knees," I answered him jokingly.

"All right, O Great One," he said, for he was always a wily fellow, never knowing how to take the moods of Fada.

"You killed a beautiful woman," he said suddenly, catching me by surprise as he spluttered out the words.

"So?", I asked, and there was uneasiness in my heart.

"So. Do you think that is blameless?"

"I am asking you."

"I will be frank with you this time Fada. But even if you were the most evil man in the world, you would still be assured of my complete loyalty and respect. I can guarantee you that there is nobody to touch you in the amount of devotion that you inspire in your followers."

"I asked you a question and not to make a speech," I shouted angrily.

"Yes and no. That is my answer."

"It is an answer I do not understand."

"Yes, O Evil One."

"What?"

He was laughing and I could see that there was some hidden meaning in what he was trying to say, but what it was I couldn't tell for the life of me. I decided to join in his laughter and I put my arm around him.

"Ho ho. I see you are still brave in the realms of thought. I would not have you any other way Pedro, for if I thought you were losing your touch, I would have you replaced immediately."

"You were right to kill her, even if she was the most perfect woman in the world."

"Why?"

"For no matter what you do, you are still the same person."

"I see. Does that answer my question?"

"It could and it couldn't. Fada, you are a great leader, but there are still some who do not understand fully the wisdom of your deeds. I have no doubt that when you sent that maid to the stake, you were aware of her courage and her beauty; even as she burned in the flames, you could see her gentleness and her truthfulness."

"Indeed that is so."

"Then for you to have punished her for her supposed misdeeds regardless of these rare qualities, shows your great capacity for sacrifice and much singleness of mind. You are a man who is unique in our time."

"Pedro. You are my judge and my friend."

The Spaniard was a wise man in his own way. If only he had been taller in size he might have commanded more success in life. We never found out if his abandoned wife ever had a child; in fact we were never to hear of her again or since, but Pedro has boasted to me that he believes one of his descendants is Voltaire, the great French thinker. He believes that the courage and the wit of the Frenchman comes from himself.

We came down from the mountains and found ourselves in another country. This new land was very pleasant, wine being abundant and the weather warm. The men began to sing again, and they were encouraged in this by the native peoples along the way, who were most cheerful and happy in their way of life. We learnt many unusual songs and heard so many different languages that I wondered what kind of a place it was we were in at all. In any case, everyone, friend and foe alike, agreed that when it came to the crunch, the speech of Fada was the finest they had ever heard. I could not be outspoken, outshouted, or outwitted.

Above all, when I came to deliver an old song of Ireland, it was agreed that Fada could not be outsung, not even by all the choirs in the land put together.

We had many discussions with the Italian chieftains, who brought along dancing girls for our entertainment. It was agreed at our first meeting that we liked one another and that there should be peace between brothers. I told them of my purpose in their land. I asked them if they thought that I might bring harm to them. This question caused great confusion among them and they spent a long time trying to decide what to answer. They replied yes, that they had some fear as stories had come before me, about my deeds; that some of their people were in great suspense. They would bow down before my authority and would grant me generous tributes. They would give me more than they ever even gave to Rome, but they pleaded with me to leave them with something of their previous possessions and not to take all of their people.

"Pile up in a heap what you have to offer; I will be generous with you all," I told them.

"Tell us, Conqueror, why you left your own land and have come such a great distance eventually to our's."

"The story of that is glorious and sad at one and the same time. In the land of Eire I was a loved and respected king. My power was great and everyone wished to live under my rule. My possessions were innumberable: herds of cattle that took up all the space in the countryside, huge houses, chattels of slaves and women, friends and a great kingdom. One day I decided that all this was too small and I set out to conquer some new places immediately. This was done and I was happy for a time. Then, with the chief minister or Tanaiste as we call him, I went up to the top of a mountain, which was the highest one in Ireland. My kingdom is wide but it needs to be wider, I said to him. I am not satisfied.

My good minister turned to me and said in as consoling a voice as he could draw up:

"Your Lordship, it can be no wider as it runs the length and breadth of Ireland and there is nothing left but the sea."

"Ah, that was a sad thing for you," they agreed.

"So it was then that I decided to set out and conquer new lands."

"You did a wise thing and we hope you go on further to conquer even newer lands," they said.

Vats of wine, hoards of silver, white horses from Arabia, chariots and fruit they piled up and offered to me.

"I will accept your gifts and long may your land retain its fertility," I said to them.

"Goodbye Fada, Great soldier, and long may you retain your luck."

Later on, Pedro said to me:

"Fada listen. The men are anxious about going on to Rome and seeing the Pope. They are concerned about the high living that goes on there. They say that his way of life is sinful and against charity. They say that people must turn away from the World and read the bible."

"Pedro, how can we read the bible when it is found only in the churches and monasteries?"

You will all remember that the discovery of printing had not yet taken place; it was in fact just being made around that time.

"They speak bitterly among themselve," was Pedro's warning.

"That is too bad. It seems to me to be an awful lot of words for men of their intelligence to have put together. In. any case, I have no interest in a religious argument. Let us get a move on."

We came to the outskirts of the City. I had Pedro advise me on etiquette, but it turned out that none of it would be necessary. A messenger was sent in to deliver our greetings. He came back out again a week later with a Roman gentleman.

"The Pope wants to know if you are a Christian," said the Roman.

"A what?"

"A ... Christian. You know, swear loyalty to the hierarchy, pay your taxes, help to repair the roof on the monastery buildings and so on."

"I have not come here to work for him, tell him."

"No, no, that is not what it means. It's ... like, have you been converted by the sword of the Muslims? Are you a Turk in disguise? Or worse still, are you Jewish? It's easy to answer his questions, you know."

"What does he want me to say? I don't understand."

"You are not from India or China. That is certain. He can tell by looking at you. Just say you are a Christian, that is the easiest. Or say you are an Irish Christian, as your messenger has just explained, though that might raise problems."

Pedro was really smirking at all of this, standing behind me, looking like the Mardi Gras fairy.

"Is he a Christian himself then?," I asked the messenger.

"He is. That is why he wants to know if you are one. He has enemies."

"Well of course tell him I am a Christian. I am not his enemy."

I smiled and waved with my wrist, for if that was all that was bothering the man then he had few worries. Off went the Roman messenger and lo and behold, the Pope and his retinue came out almost immediately. He was dressed in full, plated armour but he carried no weapons, surprisingly for such a great ruler.

"A donation you have come to offer?", he asked, as the language expert interpreted it.

"No," I replied carefully.

"Your men have made a lot of litter," he replied crossly.

"They are a most powerful army," was my reply.

"Could it be," he asked after a consultation with an expert at his side and a pause for deep reflection, "that you have come here to offer your services to my ... Temporal domain? It's quite widespread." There was a pause.

"You are not by any chance thinking of going to Jerusalem to retake the Holy City? If that were so, you would be the most honoured man in Europe. You may be a few centuries late for the Crusades but you would have the element of surprise."

There was no way of deducing his real feelings about all of this for the Latin tongue and his sombre expression told me nothing.

"No."

"Are there any 'Protestors" in your army?,' he asked.

"No," I lied.

He nodded his head and then he looked at his assistant who handed him a little green book which Pedro told me later was a catechism. He opened it at a page.

"What is baptism?," he asked.

"What's the answer, Pedro?"

"Don't answer it. It's a trick question," he advised me.

I shrugged my shoulders. He asked me another question after rifling through a few pages.

"Name me the four Cardinal Virtues."

I shook my head.

He turned another page.

"The Seven Deadly Sins?"

I pretended I was perplexed.

"Who are you? Where do you come from?," he shouted.

"I am the great Fada from Ireland."

"That is where I have the worst flock in the world. Didn't they teach you anything over there? Oh, why should we bother? So you have come here to play up, to see the sights, then?"

"I can only hope that your health is not too bad. I have come here," I said with my patience beginning to wear thin, "to bring the respects of my aunt who asks for your blessing."

"Let us go back to the city," said the Pope, ignoring me There then followed a little incident that I somewhat regret now. I don't even know how it started. All I know is the Pope pushed me back with all his strength and there was a gang of us around him. There was a good deal of kicking and shoving until some officers from both sides separated us – to my relief I may add, though I acted as if I was out of control and pretended to want to get back at him. So poor aunt Aine had to do without her blessing. I said to Pedro, let us get out of here as fast as possible, for he is a holy man and there is no knowing what he might do. We went away and the men became happy again. I asked Pedro a little while later to point out those who were "Protestors" and I immediately had them put to death, by throwing them into a steep river.

My reasons for this were twofold: one being well-known to any leader, that they might soon protest against me; and also for their continual insulting of a respected, dedicated and beloved man in the person of the Pope.

In half a day we came up against the sea and I said to Pedro, what next?

# Chapter Seven

"I have been here before," said the philosopher, "but not in so good a time."

The sea sparkled and I have never seen anything so blue. I asked him when was he here and where were we. I felt calm and peaceful just sitting down by the shore as the soldiers swam in the water, shouting wildly and washing themselves.

"I was a heretic in Spain and they do not like heretics there," said Pedro; "I was worse than a Jew or a Moor to them. They said I was too clever by half and I was a danger to Spain and a curse on Christendom. This ill-will was for no reason other than that I held honest, simple, straightforward doubts about certain articles of Faith, which I still have. I am not a heathen or a propagandist by nature. I spoke of my doubts openly, in the streets and taverns of the main cities; especially in the sea-ports where I find there are always sympathetic listeners. I made the mistake of going to Madrid once. That is a place that is full of snobs. They set out after me and I had to run for my life. They were armed to the teeth with swords, knives, axes, gunshot, a dastardly invention; wolf dogs and a length of rope with which to tie me up. I reached the sea of Spain, from where I could run no further. I was awaiting my grim fate with a happy smile and the resignation only a peaceful man can have, when a strange intervention took place. They had surrounded me and I had no hope of living another minute. I heard heavenly music and I saw very far away, three angels approaching carrying swords. Everything stopped. My enemies fell on their knees and my own heart was in my mouth. They had come when they saw the persecution of a truthful man, which was me. They carried me heavenward in the safety of their arms. Across the ocean we went and I was let down on a distant shore, in what turned out to be Italy. We are on that shore now, Fada."

I thought for a long time on this tale. It was a strange story and one which lends itself neither to disproving or proving. Pedro was never one to make up stories just for the sake of it. Lies have sometimes been on his tongue, but what purpose was there in lying about such a matter as this to me? Was he trying to impress me with the importance he figured he was held in up in Heaven? I do not think he believed anything like that carried any weight with me. I tended to believe him, for it is said that the southern people are predisposed to having visions. He described the incredible event in a very matter-of-fact voice that sounded as if he was speaking the truth.

A soldier came up to me and said that he had gone into town to get a few things and that while he was there, it was confidentially said to him that five armies intent on our destruction were coming our way and that if we didn't watch it, our days were up. The approaching forces knew

102

they had us trapped and they had carefully cut off all possible routes of escape.

"Now what would you do in a situation like that?"

It was not clear whom Fada had addressed this question to, or if it was meant for any one of us at all. I glanced at the tired and puzzled guests, who did not seem to be enthusiastic to answer the question the man asked. I realised that it was only remarkable self-discipline on my part, as well as sheer effort and zeal, and a few drops of the hard stuff, that maintained the progress of the proceedings. I looked at them directly, giving them a good stare. One man shrugged his shoulders after a while but said nothing. Some of them looked up at the roof. I thought it was hopeless to expect anything from them.

"I hope they cut his head off," a woman suddenly screeched to my surprise.

"And his feet too," said another woman.

I was pleased. At least they were emotionally involved.

"They had very good torture in those days," said a man, "crucifying and so on. I hope they crucified him."

"Along with that liar Pedro and the whole gang of hooligans," said yet another woman.

"Very good. But it would not do to return these compliments to Fada. Can you suggest anything as to how he might get out of such a predicament? It is only to show interest really. Say something I can tell him."

"Tell him we think it would be best for him if he were to stay and face the enemy like a brave man," somebody said.

"O.K."

"Fada, are you there? We are ready. We all wish to see you victorious in battle. Our faith in your might is such that we believe the enemy would flee at the sight of you. Stand and fight we say, and spare no one."

"It was Pedro himself who provided the solution. We needed to be lifted across the sea, not in a fleet of boats, but rapidly and in safety as Pedro had been transported years before in the arms of the messengers of Heaven. I decided that our army, our animals and all our goods would travel in this way. But miracles are not part of the way of life of an Irishman and I asked Pedro to call down his friends from Heaven. He said that it was impossible; they only might come of their own accord and no-one else's, not even Fada's.

I thought about this particular problem for a while. If they had come once before to save Pedro's life, perhaps they would come again on the same mission? I spoke to Pedro about this. It would, I said, have to be a genuine attack on you, with its purpose and putting into effect mitigated in no way. We will not hold back our spears or our blows. I got ready a plan of action for this. I explained to the men only that they were to kill Pedro. As we were about to start, Pedro took me aside and spoke thus:

"I have thought of something important. What if it was all a dream that I had and there were no angels?"

"If it was a dream, how were you saved from your pursuers?"

"Maybe a fisherman took me across."

"I do not understand this. How could you remember a dream and yet forget about an important matter such as a fisherman rescuing you by the skin of your teeth?"

"It may have been that what I thought were angels were really the fisherman's daughters."

"I have no doubt that they were angels, Pedro."

"I am not going to do it."

"It is Fada who decides what is going to be done," I reminded him.

"Is it not true that you need me to advise you? Who else can you trust?"

I suppose it was the despair of the moment that started Pedro putting a greatly exaggerated value on his role in the army of Fada, but I had to admit there was something worth pondering in his second question. So, I put my hope instead in the possibility that I might be able to jump across the water, depending on how wide it was. It would mean that I could not take my army with me, or any of my possessions, except the bag of gold which I tied securely to my insides. Carrying Pedro on my shoulder was to be the smallest of my problems. We went behind a sand dune. To my amazement, Pedro, despite his small size and the urgency and rush of the moment, had managed to accumulate all the silver, gold and other treasures and hidden them on his person.

When the men were not looking, we took off. To my relief, the sea was not as wide as we feared it might be and before we knew it, we were over to the other side. That is how we arrived in Spain, unknown and exposed to every danger and scoundrel.

★   ★   ★

"How do you feel at being back in the land of your mother and father?," I asked him.

"Nobody must know I am here. We will seek out Amerigo. Let us not waste a moment."

We came to Cadiz dressed as monks. We begged for alms along the way and this was surely a safe occupation as most people moved away when they saw us coming. It was around this time too, that I noticed Pedro was getting uppity and behaving not like the old one I knew at all.

"I will give a word in your ear, Fada," he said, "you must keep quiet. Spain is not France. Let me do the talking for a while".

I was too tired to argue and I was fed up at the loss of my great army, which even the king of Spain would have been proud of, I am sure. We were walking for ages.

"You are too slow, we will never get anywhere at this rate," he said to me.

I gave him a curse back in Gaelic that shut him up for a while. If anybody around heard it, they must have wondered what the monks were coming to.

We crept into the town at the darkest hour of night, and we were very careful not to let anyone see us, whether they be members of the police or cut-throats on the look-out for victims. We headed for the poorest and most derelict section of Cadiz. When we got there, Pedro suddenly appeared to be lost. To make matters worse, the rain began to pour down.

"It is so long since I was here, they have changed the streets."

"If we don't get inside soon, we will drown," I informed him.

"The only thing to do is to keep trying houses. One of them has to be his."

I did not think that was such a brilliant plan. He asked me if I had a better one and I said that it would be a wise thing to find an inn, but that I would never expect Pedro to agree to a good suggestion.

"Let's go along with your scheme to the bitter end," I said.

We tried about three hundred houses and in no instance was the occupier glad to be woken up at that hour of the morning. Then Pedro grabbed me and pointed to the next street. That's it, he said, l wouldn't mistake it anywhere.

"Do you know which house it is, Pedro? There are plenty of them there."

He did not reply. We tried every house again. We came to one which, Pedro said, was faintly familiar to him.

"I think this is it," he whispered.

He knocked and we waited. There was no sign of life and I again suggested going to an inn. He bent down and peered in through a crack.

"There is a light on in the back room. I can see its glow."

"Well why doesn't he come out or does he want us to stand here all night in the pouring rain? Give a loud knock this time."

"Do it yourself," said a somewhat embittered Pedro.

I gave the door a good bloody kick. It was opened in a moment by a young woman.

"What do you want?," she said. She was wearing a night gown, and was not too friendly.

"Wrong guess again, Pedro. It is all right, Madam, we were looking for someone else. You can go back to your bed and forget you ever saw us."

"Wait a minute," said Pedro.

"Madam, we are seeking an old friend of mine, by the name of Amerigo Vespucci. He knows me and I know him well. It was a long time ago. I thought he lived in this house."

"Amerigo is my husband. What do you want with him?"

"Amerigo, Amerigo," shouted Pedro and he more or less pushed his way into the house, past the baffled young lady; "it is me. I have come back."

A tall man came into the light and he too was in a dressing gown. He was very tired looking. He squinted his eyes as he tried to make out his visitors.

"Pedro. I thought you were run out of Spain years ago."

"I was, Amerigo. It is a miracle I have been able to come back here at all. How are you keeping? I see that you have taken a wife at last. I congratulate you."

"Thanks. I still don't understand what you are doing here. Weren't you supposed never to come back?"

"Forget about all that. Do you know what I have brought with me?"

"No. Listen Pedro. I will give you a cup of tea and then you will have to go. I have a few problems here that have come on me all of a sudden and I might even have to go away for a few weeks. My wife too, is not well. She is having pains."

"I am sorry to hear that."

"Would you prefer some wine?"

"Do you see that bag there? It is not old clothes and bread that is in that. Open it and have a look."

He went over and looked into the bag. Then he stared at Pedro.

"I knew that would surprise you. I'll bet you can think of a few things to do with that. Like buying a ship and so on?"

Amerigo appeared to relax after seeing the gold and precious objects and he sat down on a stool and put his head in his hands.

"Who is that fellow with you?", he asked when he looked up again.

"I am the great and mighty Fada of Ireland," I said loudly before Pedro could get in a word, for I was a bit annoyed at having being ignored up to this.

"He is an Irishman I met in Paris. He is all right. Don't mind him," said Pedro.

I could hardly believe it when they proceeded to discuss other matters, once again ignoring me. I was so cold and miserable after all the rain and the walking and the messing about of Pedro that I just sat down and gladly accepted the hot cup of tea that was offered to me. It did me good and I gurgled it up and down my throat making such a noise that they had to stop talking and look at me. I listened to the voice of Amerigo as he carried on a long-drawn-out conversation with Pedro. It was a very queer voice. After a while, Pedro came over to me and said that there was a bed for me at the top of the house.

I was happy to get the chance for a rest and my old friend came up the stairs with me. Once we were in the tiny room, which had no windows and was quite a come-down from what I was used to, he whispered urgently in my ear.

"Amerigo is a man who has some very old fashioned attitudes. I am surprised to see that he has a woman about the place. Don't swear in front of him Fada and above all, don't say anything offensive about women. Will you do that? Please."

"Pedro. Will you go back down to your friend and leave me in peace?"

He went off and I put my head down on a pillow that I am sure was flea-infested and before I went to sleep, I said a prayer that I would dream of the old days.

★   ★   ★

It was in the middle of the next day when I woke up and I felt as groggy as a man who had been drunk the night before. I didn't want to move at all and I had no interest in going downstairs to meet anybody. In the end Pedro came up to get me out of bed.

"Are you dead or what? Come on down, there is a dinner for you," he said.

They were seated at a table laden with dishes of food when I went down. Amerigo was smiling at me and he asked if I had a good rest.

I ate with relish, for I was very hungry.

"Tell me," says Amerigo, "what life is like in Ireland. Are the people happy?"

"Happy? yes, they are happy all right. They are happy to pray and happy to kill their enemies. Sometimes they are happy to kill a friend. They are happy to rob their neighbour of all that he possesses. Happy in life and happy in death."

"Are they oppressed by a great tyrant?"

"They are oppressed by the One from whom they cannot escape."

"What is his name?"

"They call him Hunger."

"I am sad to hear this story. Did he come from over the sea?"

"No. He has always been in Ireland and he will always be there. He cannot be driven out."

"I am a man who is interested in different countries. I have sought for your land on all the old globes and maps and I have read as much about it as I could find. I see that it is the last land on the edge of the known world. Do you know what they used to call it in the days of the Greeks? The Armpit of Hercules, I believe it translates as."

I looked over at Pedro with impatience for I could not see what this strange man was getting at with his mad talk. Pedro then interrupted the discussion with some words of his own.

"Amerigo is a scholar who is making it his business to put the whole world on a map. That is why we are going to get a ship very soon."

"Map. What is that? I have never seen one."

"Come into this room in the back and you will see one," said Amerigo loudly and with much enthusiasm in his voice. I got up from the table and followed him into the room. As we went in, I couldn't help noticing his ragged clothing and a smell that came from him. There were multitudes of paper about the place and when I asked him what they were, he said that these were the "maps". I need not add at this point that what we now refer to as paper was in those days known as parchment.

He fiddled around with some of these at a very high desk and then he said,

"Ah. Here it is. Ireland."

He beckoned me with a nod to come over.

"Ireland is here," he said.

"I thought it was a thousand miles away," was my answer.

"What he means," said Pedro who had followed us in, "is that this is a map and Ireland is drawn in with ink in a certain position. He has tried to make its shape like Ireland. Have a look at it."

I bent down and saw this sheet with a whole lot of colours on it.

"It has shrunk in size since I left."

"You will have to make an attempt to understand these things Fada, for it will be necessary to know them if we are to sail to the New World," Pedro said.

"Will you come back in here, your dinners are getting cold," shouted the wife of Amerigo from the next room. I was glad that someone in the house as well as myself, had some sense.

"Would you like to come out for a walk with me?", said Amerigo later on in the day, "it is a beautiful old city we have here and I would have pleasure in showing you around it."

"As there is nothing else to do, I suppose I won't lose anything by having a look at the sights," I answered.

Pedro said he didn't want to go and anyway he had some reading to do; so it was just Amerigo and myself who went out into the streets.

"This is a very old sea-port. I think its future is only beginning however. There are more ships in the harbour here now than I ever saw in Florence, and the ships are increasing in number every day. In a short time there won't be room for them in the water. It is my opinion that the future prospects for sea-travel are the greatest on the Atlantic sea-board and they are less so on the Mediterranean. If I were in the merchandise business, I would have my ships and my ware-house out here. This is where the future is."

I listened to him talk, for I reasoned to myself that he was one of those individuals who it sometimes is worth listening to, for the unusualness of what they say.

"I have spent my whole life in study. I have sought out all that has been written about the world by travellers. And there is nobody who knows more about maps than me. I have talked to sailors and listened to their stories and descriptions of where they have been. Every week I seek out a newly-returned ship and I go into the inn where the seamen are drinking and relaxing after their long voyage and I chat to them. I am up-to-date on all the latest developments in the world of the sea. There is very little going on that I don't know about and that is not too bad for a man who is on the shore all the time."

"Let me see me some of these men of the sea. Where are they?", I asked.

"There in an old and favourite cafe of mine that is quiet and I know the proprietor. We will go there."

We went down this steep street passing many people who were coming up. I remarked to Amerigo on the colour of their faces and he said that it was due to being in the sun for a long time and to the sea-spray. Most of them were carrying loads and I was told that they were just after getting off their ships. I could see the tops of the boats in the harbour, in which direction we were proceeding.

"Hello Amerigo, how is your wife?", were the words of the man in the cafe to my companion.

"We are both very well, thanks. To tell you the truth, a bit of good luck has come my way and to say I am on top of the world wouldn't be putting it strongly enough. It won't be long now, Juan, until I am going on that trip."

Juan, as he was called, had a laugh at this.

"How many times have you said that before, my friend. But if perseverance and dedication are enough to get you to where you want to go, you will get there in the end."

"This is my friend from Ireland. Give him a drop of wine and show him that the hospitality of us Cadizians is as good as he says it is in Ireland. Let us not be seen to be lacking in the treatment of a stranger in our midst," and Amerigo put his hand on my shoulder as he said these words, shaking me with pleasure in his eyes.

I sipped my wine and to my surprise I saw that Amerigo Vespucci was drinking only tea, a concoction that had become very popular in those days. Juan the barman went over to some new people who had come in and Amerigo told me that these were sailors.

"How do you know," I asked him, "that monsters do not inhabit these lands across the sea? How do you know that if we set out on the great ocean, we will not become lost forever in it, never seeing land again?"

"You ask wise questions Irishman"

"My wisdom and strength is known in many countries. Pedro will tell you."

"Of that I am in no doubt. Have you ever heard of Christopher Columbus?"

"The name rings a bell in my head."

"I expect Pedro has mentioned his name now and again. I do not speak to Columbus any more. He is a glory-seeker. He will bring evil in his wake. I fear that with Spanish ships and Spanish might he will discover the New World and woe betide any poor people who live there. He is an adventurer who seeks gold and booty above all else. I do not think he has a single ideal or moral principle."

I called for more wine, listening to the strange words of Amerigo in my ears.

"I have told Columbus many times that I am certain there is a new continent out there. He laughed in my face and said I was a useless idealist. The world is round I said, not flat. He laughs and says that many loonies agree with me. He is going out on the ocean to plunder and murder in the lands of Asia; what he does not know is that he will come to a brand new and unspoilt continent first."

The wine was so strong that I was finding it difficult to keep my eyes and ears attentive to Amerigo Vespucci. The noise and laughter of the sailors across at the other table also came to my ears.

"A New World," I said, "you know that it is there? Pedro has said the same thing to me. And yet none of you have seen it."

"You are truly a clever man, Fada. You are wordly-wise. You do not believe everything and anything that stray strangers put in your ear, but you ask for proof. Have you ever heard of the saying 'The Proof of the Pudding is in the Eating'?"

"The proof of the pudding is in the eating," I repeated his words.

"It is true that I have never seen this land, nor have I met any man who claims he has been there. But the mind is a wonderful thing and one is able to draw all kinds of conclusions. It is in the nature of man to progress. The first people drowned in the sea until they discovered the raft. Now look at them: they can travel in their thousands in ships that do not need oars, but are powered by the wind. Anyone who said years ago that we would be able to go across to Africa or Asia without moving a muscle, but wining and dining at our leisure while the wind did all the work, would not have been believed. In the same way now, I will make a forecast. Man cannot fly yet like the birds. Well I will prophecy that one day he will fly; not just one man alone but men in their hundreds and thousands in great big flying machines that will encircle the world. I will go farther and bet you that he will fly to the moon and beyond and then return back to earth. It will find the moon to be barren of life and the stars to be burning masses. Space is a vacuum and it is the largest ocean of all."

Amerigo shouted his words and waved his arms. His excitement was great and a dark red colour came over his face to my wonder. I could see that each person in Juan's cafe was astonished by Amerigo or expressed disagreement with him.

"Ha. I get carried away by my visions. People laugh at me. You cannot blame them, I suppose. Anyway, the old stories and legends speak of this continent. I believe it is out there, between Europe and Africa on one side, and Asia on the other. I have drawn up a map of the world with this unknown continent included. When I finished it and took a good look at it, I was astonished at how logical and simple the whole thing was. It was then that I became fully convinced. Every continent is exactly similar. It has three parts. At its extremities it is cold and frozen over. White bears and icebergs are there. In its middle part is the great temperate climate, which has none of the extremes of heat or cold that the other ends have. Your land Fada, as well as our's here, is a temperate land. Then there is a desert and in the south, a hot land of great forests and strange animals."

Amerigo stopped his talk for a while and took a sip from his tea jug.

"Aah, it is cold," he said. He waited to get his breath back again.

"When I said the proof of the pudding was in the eating, I meant that by going there and seeing this land we will be at the same time getting the proof of it. I have also pondered on the kind of people who will live there. I think they will be natives of Asia. They would have travelled there from a westerly direction, as the ocean on this side is perhaps too wide. It is most likely now that they will be widely dispersed, so that there are many different tribes who speak different languages. It could be that some of them will have developed advanced civilizations, with similarities I would imagine to the Egyptian and Persian cultures. Of course I am speculating wildly now and I would not be so confident in my predictions here. However, I would guess and guess is the word, that the majority of these tribes are at a low level of technical development in relation to our's, and some will be quite barbarous. Such is the nature of man, you know, that while some prosper, others will always come to ill."

He was quite a talker. I called for more wine for a strange thing had come to my notice concerning it. It was a wine the like's of which I had never drank before; it gave me a painful headache even as I drank it, and the only way to escape the pain was to keep sipping it; for as soon as I stopped and put it aside for a moment the pain asserted itself with a vengeance; it was relieved only with new wine.

"I hope I am not boring you with my plans," said Amerigo;

"I am not going to rob people or force my beliefs on them or make them take up my way of life," he continued, "there is too much of that going on nowadays. Our leaders in Europe are really brigands you know. Good and gentle people – there are such around even though it is hard to believe – are robbed of their possessions and are taken from their homes at night. They see their wives, their mothers and their daughters raped in front of their eyes by 'loyal' armies. They are told that they deserve everything they get, that they are bad and should not have been born. It is the weakest and most simple of souls who have been made to suffer. The wicked prosper. The poor cry out for bread and they get none. All gold and treasure accumulates to the rich. That is what life is like in Europe."

I asked him what we would do to the people whom we would find in the New World.

"We will not do anything to them. Not one thing. We will tell them that we have come to live in peace with them and that they have nothing to fear from us. We will go about our business and not interfere in their's. By our example, the usefulness of our tools and the contentment and happiness of our way of life, peace will prevail. Where land has to be shared, it will be shared. There will be no violence. Every tribe and colour will have equal shares. If a man from one tribe wishes to marry a woman from another, he will be free to do so."

He stopped talking again and gathered in his breath in a gulp for a loud statement;

"This will not happen if Columbus gets there first."

I think these were the last words I heard. They are certainly the last ones I remembered, for I collapsed off my chair on to the floor. I am told that Amerigo had to enlist the help of the sailors in the cafe to help him carry me home.

★ ★ ★

For three days I stayed in my bed and did not come downstairs. I saw Pedro, who also brought me soup.

"Between you and me," he said, "Amerigo is angry about what has happened. It did not do him any good in front of all those people. He does not agree with drinking, much less with drinking to excess. Everybody saw you being carried through the streets."

"What do I care about Amerigo Vespucci? He is nothing to me."

"He is like a brother to me. He is a good friend to have. You would be fortunate to be able to claim him as a friend, Fada."

"What, me, Fada?", I laughed at him.

"Yes, you Fada. Do you see that woman down there? She shares his meals and his bed. Well, he found her as a tramp. She sold her wares along by the waterfront of Cadiz. She did not know any other life before Amerigo found her and took pity on her. He married her to prevent her going back to her old way of life. Marriage is just a hindrance to him in his plans. But that is the way with Amerigo. His own wishes come last."

"I am sure he is a holy man, Pedro, and that you respect him for that. But how has he made his living, for pure motives and a clean character are not yet sufficient to provide a man with bread and butter?"

"He is a map-maker. It is a new art and he sells them to ships' captains."

"What is map-making?"

"It is the drawing of places on parchment. It is done with a heavy dye. Lines are put on old bark or leather fragments and these lines are supposed to be the coasts and rivers and mountains of lands that the ships are to visit. He obtains accurate descriptions of these places from sailors and captains who have been there and he can improve on them after each voyage. He is constantly revising and improving his maps."

"I do not understand. Why are these pictures necessary to a captain?"

"They tell him the direction in which to go in order to reach a place. They tell him the distance he has to travel. They help him to guide his ship in treacherous harbours. Maps have put the bible out of date, Fada; they are the bibles of the future."

"And what are our plans?", I asked him with resignation, for it was all a bit much for me.

"We will buy a ship. And we will need a crew and men who will come with us to the New World and help us with our ventures there. This is where we will have to be very careful, as it is in the recruitment of our crew that lie the seeds of failure or of success. I have a few ideas of my own here, Fada, that we must see to it are put into effect. None of our men must be wise in the art of war. They should have no tendency to talk or dispute. If a man shows a wish to question or to talk back, he must not be taken on. If we have even one man with us, who possesses an individual personality, or has courage or ambition, he would be worse than the plague and it would be the end of everything. Instead, they will show a great desire to keep quiet and get on with the job. The swinging of axes against trees, the smashing of fire wood, digging of the soil, contentment in the noises of birds and of the jungle and displeasure in the society of humans; that will be their talent. They will be warned beforehand that there is to be no return. For the purpose of our sailing then, we will require sailors who have no homes to return to, and who would relish the thought of vanishing into the sea."

"I have been on the sea before," I told him, "and it seemed that the water would swallow up the ship and everyone in it. There was a great fear in me at the time."

"Is that so?", asked Pedro with some surprise.

"I closed my eyes and shut the door of my cabin for I had no wish to go out and tempt the vastness of the ocean."

"That is like the elephant who was afraid of the mouse," said Pedro, "there is nothing to worry about."

I thought it was a bit funny, the sight of Pedro trying to give encouragement to Fada.

"Do you think I am afraid?", I asked him.

"No," he replied

"The sea," Pedro went on, "is a blessing to mankind. It was put there to enable him to escape. I believe this is its chief function. Look at how many escapes there have been in history across the great oceans. How many people and tribes have been rescued from slavery, oppression and death by the freedom of the waters?"

★ ★ ★

One evening, over cups of wine and tea in the cafe, the two of them said to me:

"You sit here brooding and fuming like a dragon. The day does not stay for any man and we must prepare ourselves for what is ahead of us. In the past you were a lion. You were a shark in the ocean. Now you must become as quiet as a bat in a cave; you must be as gentle as a skylark in the heavens. Your mighty face is as red as blood and as mountainous as the mountains, but you must make it as peaceful as are the fertile plains and as smooth as water. Your hands of iron that have subdued a thousand men must become as soft and as soothing as those of a woman. Listen to us Fada, and the world will be our's to do what we will with it."

Amerigo went to do something in the back of the building and I asked Pedro, who still wore the guise of a holy monk that we had come in, to get me more wine. I felt very bad. When they spoke thus to me, heavy sleep came into my eyes and there was an ache in my head. I felt they were staring at me and I thought there was a funny look on their faces. Uneasy feelings ran through my blood. My own tongue seemed to have lost its own powers and I imagined I had become frozen, like water in the wintertime, for I was stiff and unable to move. I could hear their words going round and round in my head. I was glad when Pedro pushed same wine in front of me.

"He is an extremely nice man, don't you agree?",asked Pedro referring to Amerigo.

"Yes, he is a courteous man and one I think you can trust. Let us be gone to this new place for I would like to rest my feet and raise some cattle. I am tired of galavantings. My red beard has lost its gloss and my clothes are becoming old and tattered. Let us get away from the towns and cities, where the talk of the people sounds like the clatter of hailstones on roofs; whose schemes are wicked and their wish but to rob their friend."

"That is nothing but the truth," said Pedro.

"Pedro, what is the month and the year?"

"It is the month of May and the year is fourteen ninety one."

"Make way for this old gentleman," cried Amerigo as he came back in with his arm around an old sailor.

"Let this seaman of countless storms take a seat and rest his weary bones. We are going to make a bargain with him."

A white-haired aged man sat down beside me and he immediately grabbed the bottle of wine from the table and began slugging it back. He finished all that was in it in one go.

"He is going to sell his ship to us," said Amerigo, "he is very fond of it but we are offering a good price."

"I am Captain Rodriques," said the seaman, "and I will sell my ship for a good price in gold, as dear as it is to me. I think this Amerigo is crazy if he sails to where he says he is going to, but that is his business. I would advise you, if you are his friends, to persuade him to another course. There are monsters in that sea, great big things that come up in the night and suck men overboard. I have seen them myself. They have fire in their eyes and are as large as mountains. They have no mercy and they swallow up whole ships."

# Chapter Eight

"On Earth our paths came to be intertwined and I do not know why or how it was so. Fada and I were like the coming together of the rambling pathway and the rushing stream; of the moon and the sun; of wild forests and rolling plains, cultivated gardens and waterfalls. We have been joined as a hurtling meteor and a burning star as we plummet down through the void."

It sounded like Pedro speaking, although the voice was hoarse and unnatural, as a sad man's is. It was the voice of one who was trying to give eloquence to sorrow and deeply sad thoughts, and who did not have much faith in his words as he did so.

"Death has been well-known throughout history. It is not necessary to inform even a schoolboy of it, is it? You see it everywhere around you. Anywhere you may care to look. It comes to the old and to the young. The dumb and the enlightened must welcome its embrace at one time or another. The birds and the slugs in the ground say goodbye to the world. Even the weed dies."

"A grand speech," I interrupted, for my listeners were becoming oppressed by the words of Pedro and I did not think he was doing anything to help raise the lagging spirits. The patience and forbearance of them was not at its best; but at the same time I did not want the philosopher to start getting upset and feel that his contribution was not being appreciated.

"A speech full of wisdom and common sense."

"Fada and I have many discussions on this subject and I am sorry to say that the man is beginning to doubt my word. He is beginning to disbelieve the facts of life. It is a bad sign. He asks me how long do we have to stay around here; it seems to be an eternity already to him. He complains that we have nothing to concern ourselves with. All we can do in observe the ant-like activities of mankind down below, whose deeds we do not influence. In the end, he says, it would be better to try the doors. I am afraid his mind is beginning to turn in that direction now, despite my assurances that our patience will be rewarded. Let him get on with his yarn and do not give him any bad advice. He is like a little child, or worse, an old man, rambling on about great deeds and fairytale places with the illusions that the span of four centuries can give to anything. You can imagine. He still tries to live as he once did; drinking the wine of long-extinct barrels and trying to perform the Lame for long-extinct audiences. I will return to my (need I tell you?) imaginary library now, for he is about to return from a spin around nowhere, if he would admit it."

"Fada was given the task of collecting together a sea-worthy crew of loyal sailors who would give up all that they had, even their right arms, for the privilege of treading in unknown waters and the possible honour of losing their lives in the sinking ocean."

Fada was speaking in improved and more optimistic tones. The walk may have done him good. Outside, the stars glided over us and the world dipped its wings in the heavens. I looked to see if there was any sign of the pale light of dawn, but the night was still full.

"To look for these men who would prove to be trustworthy and obedient souls, I did not go to the seaside shops and cafes of the waterfront where sailors wise in the ways of ships and the world were wont to loll around; for Pedro said that those would be hard to control, by being mutinous and faithless during the voyage, especially when hardships arose, as they were bound to. It is a fact, he said, that a true sailor goes berserk should he not have the opportunity to rob and kill, to rape and loot frequently. In most cases, craziness overcame them regardless, at regular intervals.

Instead I went out to the country and picked up ten of the quietest and most harmless individuals you could expect to meet in the course of a very long walk and a very long day. By wellsides and trees, rivers and gateposts they hung about, without fear or favour, with nothing of possessions and even less with which to occupy themselves. When I told them of the great journey ahead, of its risks and attendant possible rewards, such as escape from boredom and drudgery, their replies were detached and of a manner that can only be said to be philosophical. Neither did they show any hesitancy when I told them that they were going where no men had gone before, and that it was unlikely they would be coming back. To each one I gave a sum of money, with instructions to turn up at the pier on the date of our leaving, which was two days ahead. It was to cause much trouble and consternation later, that these recruits had no knowledge of boats or water. However, all that was still ahead of us and on the morning of the voyage we celebrated our coming departure in the house of Amerigo Vespucci. Juan had come along and he brought with him a large number of bottles of wine, which he offered to me as a parting gift.

"The wine is vinegar. I hope it is better in the land to which we are going. I will take them anyway."

Amerigo introduced Pedro to Juan as Dom Peter, a monk of the Order of Saint Peter from the Basque, who was to be the spiritual adviser on the journey. It had came to my notice already that Pedro was careful never to make an appearance on the streets of Cadiz unless he was garbed in that cloak.

Pedro had insisted that no women were to accompany us on the voyage, as that would only lead to trouble between the men. You could not even trust your wife in a situation like that, he told Amerigo, at the same time making a covert reference to her past occupation. So it was presumed that he would be leaving the woman behind; and it was to our great surprise that we saw Amerigo handing over the keys to his house to Juan, to whom he had just sold it. I think Pedro and I were too busy and preoccupied at the time to ask him where she was. It is little wonder that on the hour of our sailing, when glory and pleasure should have surrounded us, there was delay and ineptitude aplenty so that in the end, we were not able to set out at all. It was a time of shame as the crowds who had come down to the shore to laugh at us and to mock us when we were first preparing the ship, were now given ample opportunity to extend their revelry and to increase their mirth. In the end, it was Amerigo alone who took the ship out into the open ocean. By the time the front of our boat was put facing the horizon and our backs had been turned on all land, I was setting about learning the arts of sea-faring and becoming a sailor. But it was then that the swelling and the tilting of the ship on the sea began to cause me more distress that it is possible to imagine. I was immediately sorry that I had ever come on the voyage and I asked Pedro to tell Amerigo to turn back. He came back with the message from the captain that it was still possible for me to swim back, providing the sharks did not get me first. I was too ill and distressed to do anything about this message.

It was early in the voyage too that I was informed by Pedro of the great fear in which I was held by the crew. This did not surprise me, for they were creatures who should never have been born. Pedro suggested that I stay in the lower deck, preferably in my own cabin, and that this would kill two birds at the same time; it would help my sea-sickness and also calm the crew.

What of that so-called loyal and brave crew? The fame of my deeds and strength had come to their ears and they trembled in my presence. This gave me satisfaction. It also gave me satisfaction that I was able to frighten them by grabbing their legs as they walked past the grill of my cabin window. However, I decided that I would tolerate them and not throw them into the sea, which shows you what a changed man Fada was. They did not cause fights or indulge in cursing or drinking. Their heads they kept bowed much of the time, as though they feared being upbraided by someone; they ceaselessly walked about, afraid to be still for a second in case something happened. The look in their eyes was such that you would think they expected the sky to fall down at any moment.

Pedro came down to my cabin one day, saying he had come to enquire about my health, but I could see that he was in a terrible huff. He could barely restrain his anger.

"Fada, how are you? I am sorry I have not come to see you more often but I have been a busy man. I need not tell you, up in my quarters I have been thinking about what we will do in the New World and what we will find there. We will be free there, that is the best thing of all."

"I was thinking myself," I said, "that you would have been spending your time hearing confessions and saying prayers."

"That is it," he shouted angrily, "that is just it. Do you know what Amerigo has done? Do you know what the stinking rat has done?"

It was a strange sight to see Pedro cursing and shouting in the monk's garb.

"What has he done?", I asked with wonder.

"He brought a priest aboard unknown to us all. I happened to see him going about his ministerial duties by chance, for he does it in the late hours when they think I am always asleep. He sneaks around the men's cabin hearing their confessions and giving spiritual counsel. I could not believe my eyes."

"What does it matter Pedro? Perhaps the men need a priest. Perhaps Amerigo believed they would not have travelled if no priest had been there to give them comfort. What concern is it of our's?"

"I am sorry that you have become like this, Fada. Where is that greatness of your's that threatened half the world and had mothers and widows crying after their menfolk? It is sad now to see the weak state of your will, which used to be as strong as a storm, and is now like a wisp of straw in the sea. Awake, Great Fada; our enemies surround us once again. Look. Their plottings are written in the sky. The dreadfulness of their deeds is as certain as is falling rain after thunder. We must fight them, or they will destroy us."

"You are a funny man, Pedro. Tell Amerigo that I am getting old and that I desire rest. Give him my wish that he will guide this ship to land soon. Make peace with that priest, Pedro, and join your powers to his so that you may both benefit mankind. Send him down to me too, as there are matters I desire to confess to him."

The philosopher of Spain looked at me as though I had become possessed by the devil. He pulled his lips inward and his eyes went wild. It was a sight and a half. The state of him then would surely have made him a fit companion of any devil.

"There are going to be innocent people in the New World, Fada. They will be free of all the barbarous customs of Christians. Now I do not think that priest is going to be content with the small parish he already has here on the boat. He will have designs on our new-found brethren also. He will want to be another Apostle. He will desire the expansion of Mother Church. He will contaminate them with false doctrines. Fada, you are still a mighty and a great one. You are greater by far than Amerigo. The Lame is your immortal feat. Show the priest its secret. He will grab at anything that will increase his power. Let him try the great jump on the deck. Everybody up there is bored stiff for the lack of amusement. I will work it so that you can come up to do it. Tell him that he too can learn this great act. He will go up in the air and when he comes down, the ship will already be gone and he will land in the sea. It is a fair way of disposing of a vagabond. Listen and heed my words, Fada, and you will be great again."

"That which you suggest is murder."

"It is," he replied straightforwardly.

"Is that not wicked?"

"It is a wicked deed in a wicked world."

"Then I will not do it. I have no wish to be a murderer."

"You are already a murderer many times over."

"It may be that I have killed in the past. Then I was a murderer, but I am no longer one."

"You have learnt something after all. I was beginning to think it was a hopeless case."

"I would murder a hundred thousand people more easily that I would a priest. Go and do it yourself, Pedro, and be warned beforehand that when it is done, I will inform Amerigo who was the perpetrator, and you will be hanged."

"It has all been due to your example, who once demolished people like the bricks of an old house. I am not going to talk to you again."

The poor fellow. So much for his not speaking to me, he would put his head in the door or through the window very often after that, to issue warnings, what he called "good advice" and even threats. One day he even went as far as to say that my bag of gold, which was my only possession, was not entirely safe and there could be individuals about who had their eyes on it.

Loud were my shouts to be released from this tiny cabin, whose uncomfortableness was worse than all the terror in the ocean.

The badness of my stomach which had originally caused me to go down to the bottom of the ship, was gone and I shouted to be released at once. At last Amerigo came down and he spoke to me in a quiet and sincere manner.

"I have not forgotten you, Fada. I will never forget you."

"Let me out now, Amerigo. My legs are stiff and I have lost my terror of the sea."

"You have always been free to do as you please, my good friend. You may walk the deck as you please, when you please, where you please. You will do so in chains however, for there is no knowing when the treacherous ocean might come in and attempt to drag you off. It is as unpredictable as the fury of a woman, and as merciless as a thousand vandals. You will be safer in chains."

"I do not doubt your wisdom in these matters, Amerigo. Woe betide the day that anything should happen to you, for if Pedro were in charge of this ship we would sail right into Hades. Only you can bring us all safely to the New World."

"The stars in the sky are different and the sun goes yet higher still with the passage of each day. You will find it a changed world up on the deck, for we have moved through great distances. We are going into the centre of the world."

"It makes me tremble again to think of the nature of our enterprise."

"When all is calm up there, and the wind is quiet and there is no danger of a deluge of rain, you will be brought up for a breath of fresh air."

"I can hardly thank you enough for that, Amerigo. Who else can I trust now?"

Some days later, I was led up to the deck and the glare and heat of the sun made me cover my eyes to protect them from the pain; for they found it difficult at first to look on any object. What colour is the sea? I have seen colours I can never describe, not if I live a thousand years. The waters were purple and red, green and blue, black and white at the same time. I could not tell the sea from the air, or the waves from the clouds. Our ship seemed to be sailing through the open sky. I clung to the deck and to posts for fear of falling, and I did not know what it was into which I would fall. How many words did I speak to the sea? Deep and unfathomable though was its reply. It spoke of ghosts, hidden down below and longing to be free so that they might take flesh. I listened intently to their cries. There were many of them and I was sure that the terror of their appearance would be the death of the world. I commanded the sea to hold them down and so be worthy of the honours of men.

Then, as if at a signal the gods had been notified of the return of Fada to the open world, a storm broke out that filled the sea and the sky with a roar and a deluge of water came down upon us. Many things were shown to my sight in that hour, as the depth below threw up all that it possessed. I saw demons and monsters and my eyes were astonished. Terrible creatures arose like giant snakes, to devour us and our ship."

This storm of Fada's caused havoc and consternation in the room and it was only my grim determination that prevented the audience from running out of the place altogether. I did not want to lose any witnesses to what I considered as being my greatest achievement yet. Loud thunder claps were heard by us all and flashes of ghostly lightning ripped around us. People fell off their chairs and the table was lifted up from the floor. Many things tumbled and crashed. I found myself being thrown from my own eminent position at the head of the table, to a sitting position at the far end of the room.

★   ★   ★

I could hear Amerigo giving commands in lofty and calm tones from the top deck. Then I saw Pedro running around. He was like a lost sheep and he was glad to see me, for he laughed and put his arms on my shoulder. He asked me if I was noticing the manner in which the ship was sloping and how much water there was on the deck already. Amerigo, he said, was worried and was hoping for a miracle.

"The calmness of Amerigo will bring us through this terrible storm," I told him, "for is there not wisdom and strength in his voice as he gives his commands? Listen to his voice; it carries through the wind and the rain. He will not fail. And if he does, we need not weep, for we will all be together in our destruction, and we will have one another for company as we sink to the bottom of the sea."

He said to me; Fada, who will save the ship if Fada cannot? He asked me; who was greater than Fada in this world and both of us agreed that no one was. I said to him that a word from Fada will be louder than the loudest thunderclap and the sky above would become as meek as a child. The soft voice of the man of Ireland will cool the angry fear on the distraught face of the heavens. Trouble yourself not, I told him; as the look in my eye is sharper than any stroke of lightning and is fiercer at the same time. When I spoke thus also to Amerigo, calm and wonder came over his face and he said these words:

'Fada will be for the deliverance of us all.' It was then that he wept.

Fate was in the hands of Fada, whose judgement the swirling waters awaited. I said these words to Pedro:

"Let the holy cleric be respected to walk about his business. Let not a finger be laid on him, if the hand of doom is not to come down on you and everyone. Take no weapons to curb him, nor use words against him. Suffer him in silence and do not hamper him.

A promise from a philosopher is as seldom as a sunburst in the night and a promise from a philosopher was a price for the salvation of us all. There was grievous sorrow in Pedro at my words and a fist of anger he pushed in my side. My laughter was in his wounds. He pleaded as does a dog in pain. More fierce did the winds and the rains become.

"If the priest's freedom is to be your price, so be it. But it is the giving away of the light of the sun for the gift of the moon," he cried.

At last I rose up my mighty voice against the heavens. A roar I sent as my messenger to the farthest reaches of the sky. In return was a terrible reply of fire and rain and thunder. With much strength, the storm and I contested. I commanded the unruly clouds to be quiet and soon they became silent and obedient. The sea returned to a gentle and normal appearance and our boat once more sailed swiftly and smoothly.

★   ★   ★

After that disturbance on the deck, I returned to my cabin for I had no wish to see ship or ocean again. Amerigo came to thank me for what I had done and, as he said, to cheer me up a bit.

"I have desired to have a heart to heart talk with you for a long time, Fada. I owe you many things and I do not think that I have always treated you fairly. Such is the injustice of life that worthy people often get the rough end of the stick. I hold you in higher esteem than I do Pedro or any other man aboard this ship. Your kind consideration in the storm will be remembered. I am glad to see that you no longer suffer so terribly from the seasickness."

"Your kind words are a help to me. There is none the equal of Amerigo Vespucci on the seas."

"Little do you know of Amerigo Vespucci."

I looked at him with surprise, for he sank to the ground at my feet and sorrow filled his eyes. He put hands to his face to cover up the tears of a strong man.

"If there is anybody who deserves to be known for the discovery of the New World, it is you Fada. If there is anybody to whom the credit of history and the praises of men are due, it is you, the wild man of Ireland. Ah, the near ending of our voyage in the recent storm, and the almost sure finishing of us all at the ocean's bottom, has opened my eyes. My name is Amerigo Vespucci but the praises that extend to it do not also belong to me. I am a jealous and vengeful rogue. I have been deceiving myself for all of my life. It is a bitter lesson to learn at this hour when so much harm has been done, that it cannot be undone. Every day when the welfare of my ship and its crew should be foremost in my mind, what am I thinking?

I am pre-occupied with the fear that Columbus will already be in the New World when we get there.

Instead of watching over my ship, I am looking out on the ocean, living in a nightmare that the boat of Columbus will appear and will pass us by. Why do my thoughts not concern themselves with the progress of this voyage and see to the many problems that are showing themselves daily? Would it not be wiser and more apt for the success of our plans to try and steer this ship swiftly and steadily, instead of occupying myself with vain plans of denigration of the name of Columbus, especially should he succeed where we fail? This is what I tell myself now."

"Who is this Columbus?", I asked, for his name was coming to sound like that of the Devil to me.

"We grew up as brothers in the city of Florence, where art and trade are honoured equally. Our parents had mighty dreams for us, but we became locked in rivalry from that time. He it was who had the most generous heart. He was the believer, while it was I who mocked even as I listened. His mind was noble and I scoffed. We went in the gardens among the young fruit trees and played in the bloom of the flowers. He said that the two of us, one day, would sail to a new land and our deeds would be remembered with gratitude for all time. Even then he knew that the world was round. I made a fool of him in front of the other boys in the school and I saw to it that he never had much peace. And I have used all that he told me; I have taken from him even his vision and his dream; and put them to serve my own honour and glory ever since. That is your Amerigo Vespucci."

He said these words in a voice that was shaking and it had become hoarse by the time he was finished. There was silence for a time, until he had recovered his voice. The man then pushed an object into my hand which he told me was his compass with his name etched on it. It was his gift to me and a memento that he hoped would always be very valuable to me. He hugged me and said that without my help he would not be where he was now. He said he had a small favour to ask of me.

"On the day we sail into shore, it is my wish that you stay on the ship and not put foot on land. The protection of this vessel against treacherous attack is the task that I have appointed to you."

With that, he walked out of the cabin, without waiting for my question and pausing only to step over my legs.

The chiefest of surprises that occurred to me on that boat was the unlikely pleasure of making friends with one of the crew. I had become more interested in their activities and I studied them from the window. They worked as quietly as kittens and never strayed near my cabin. The odd shout I gave, to encourage them, for their despair was for all to behold; or to invite back a friendly reply, for we were alone together on the same ship after all. At last my patience was rewarded and I persuaded one of them to enter into card games with me. It was a game somewhat similar to poker. We played for brass buttons, as money was scarce and our meagre possessions we agreed were too precious to lose. I talked with him and explained the various purposes of our trip. It was to my regret that I learned that neither my friend, whose name I was never able to find out, nor the rest of the crew, had any idea of where they were going, or why they were on the ship. I put many questions to him and I discovered that he could remember nothing. Few were the words of that man; slow were his hands in cards; unwieldy his head and heavy and cumbersome were the sounds of his tongue. Much talk I made in his presence, to fill the imaginings in my mind and to hide the wide and empty gaps of silence that were long in between our words. Songs and cajolery were continually on my lips.

In the darkness of the night I was visited by the priest. His features were tall and gaunt and he wore a black shroud in which was hidden his face. I could see only his eyes, which were stone-grey, and his anvil-like nose.

"You who stand there as silent as a crow in the night, you are the priest whom I have never set eyes on until now. Am I wrong?"

"You are right."

"Do not accuse me, holy man, of things I did not do and do not send me into the outer darkness."

"Why are you in the corner like that?", was his reply and his question.

"The corner is safe and I can see on all sides from it."

"I have prayed for you and for all the men on this ship. I have prayed more for you than for the others, for your gifts are great and so the burden that is on you is the greatest of all and is as heavy as ten mountains heaped up one on to another."

I did not know what to make of this talk.

"All that has been given to us may be used for good or ill. It is often as much a matter of luck or of chance that decides whether we take the right road or the wrong one. Heaven or Hell may be won and lost in the gust of a wind or the passage of a wisp in a stream. Mountains have sunk and floods overrun the world for the want of a bit of good advice."

"Many have come to me in their time and they have not gone away but as wiser men. What is it you wish to know?"

"What is this power that you have?"

I thought about this for a time and a searing anger went through my brain. It had been my hope never again to lift a finger to a man but my outrage in realising that this priest was after my gold hit me as hard as if a wall had fallen on me. It smoothened my senses. My wits left me and revenge flamed in my blood. I took him in hand and put him hanging from the roof.

"No man will ever have my gold. No man has ever set eyes on my gold. Why do you wish to possess it, for do you not have sufficient of your own? Answer me now as it is my wish to cut open your throat, which is a fate not respectable for any man, and less so for a priest."

"Let me down. It is not in my scheme to take any gold from you. That which is your's is your's and that which is mine is mine. Let me down and I will tell you the truth."

"Tell me it as you are. I would be happier to hear the truth from a man who is upside down than hear a falsehood from him standing up."

"Some told me you were a merciless tyrant. I replied to those detractors that your goodness was that of a child's and your mercy was as free as the laughter of the angels. I come to you with joy in my heart and a hope that good alone may befall you. Let me down and I will deliver my message with sincerity."

He was released and he laid his heavy hands on my shoulder. I do not think I have seen a man so calm in my life, as this priest, who was cool like the ice that never melts and quiet like the shepherd on the cold hillside. He spoke these words to me:

"There is work to be done in this new land. There is good work to be done and there is bad work that will be done, for the devil is everywhere, except in Heaven, as we are all taught. For me to sit here with you gives me strength, and the touch of my hands on you now is a source of new-found wisdom. The heathens who inhabit far-out places are wild and angry people, who know the blade and blood, but not the book and faith. I fear that they will drown the Word in orgies of shouting and war-cries and I will be speaking to the wind, if I live. For my death alone is guaranteed in the New World. The destruction of everything I have believed in and spent my life working for, is further guaranteed by the presence of Pedro the Purveyor of Untruth who will, in his determination, warp these savages permanently in the ways of the devil. Nothing can be understood in this life, except that all has been given to us for the doing of good. That alone we can know. It is a simple truth. It is the only one we need to know. If only people would believe that one simple straightforward truth; there would be no more evil."

His eyes spoke the truth also.

"Nobody knows why it is you were chosen, in the great mystery of things, to be given the gift you have, man of Ireland, and the wild power that is in your blood. Let it be put now in the service of mankind and turn aside from the falsehoods of Pedro. Come with me to the fields and villages of these new people and you will know no sorrow."

"I do not obey the commands of any man."

"Let me speak to you as a friend to a friend, a brother to a brother, a father to his son. I see you as you do not see yourself. Which of us know ourselves? Do you feel the tenderness there in your heart that I know is hidden there? My brother, my sweet and tender brother, and my son, you are both my son and my brother, how I have watched you all this time and seen so many virtues in you and it all uncherished and unsung. The truth that I say is a surprise to you, for those who are marked by God do not know it. O, do not go throwing your virtues like stones into a pond."

I assured him of the benevolent use of my powers, for I do not like to see a priest beg.

He told me his name was Paulo Marti. When he had finished his sermon, I relaxed and we got to talking about more common or garden subjects. He was able to give me some news of the voyage, which I appreciated, as I had not the slightest clue as to what was happening upstairs.

"There is a good sign. Birds fly above us and bits of land are around us; boughs and other flotsam."

"Is that a good omen?"

"It is a great sign. The discovery of such objects so far out in the ocean is a significant event, for they do not originate in the water. They have come from land which is not too far away."

"I am glad to hear that. Tell me, priest Paulo, what has led us all this way; Amerigo, the Stars, or God Above? To whom do we owe our praises and our thanks?"

"To all three. Each has led us here in their own way."

But we were not there yet. It has been agreed over the centuries by those who know best, such as seamen and scientists, that mists do not occur in those seas the ship of Amerigo had traversed; in other words, the seas of the Tropics which are hot and blue and oftentimes a silver colour in the sun. The day after this visit of the priest, we entered a mist which, spectre-like, came over our boat causing a darkness of time and spirit.

Two days after the clearance of this fog, I saw that we had come across a small boat in the water with brown-coloured men in it. It was not possible to understand how it was they had travelled out into the ocean with nothing to drive them; no sails or oars or paddles. They had few clothes on them and they were miserable in expression. However, when they were being taken aboard, they became happy and made signs showing that they wished for food and drink. I could see that so great was their joy at being able to leave their own boat, that they embraced those of our crew who helped them.

It was only one day after this that Pedro made one of his rare appearances in my room. He yawned and stretched as he always did when nervousness or anxiety overcame him. I did not let him speak first. I demanded to know why the brown-skinned men had not been brought to me. He replied that they had been stranded for weeks without food or water and they were tired.

"Do you remember," he asked, "that it was I who told you of the New World?"

"I remember as I please."

"Do you remember," he said in a changing and trembling voice, "that I said that Amerigo Vespucci was the best sea-captain in the world?"

"It was you who said that."

"I spoke of wilful and determined men who would try to turn us from our path and put snares in our way?"

"There are such men everywhere."

"I promised that there would be freedom there and no more robbing and cheating." His voice was now high with excitement.

"That promise was your's."

"The sea," I said, "would be wet and the days and nights long."

"There can be no denying that."

"That at the end the sea would finish and the land begin?"

"Yes."

"Well, look out the window, it is there."

# Chapter Nine

A great welcome was given to us all there in that sunny land. I could hear the music of conch shells in my ears and the strange trees were a sight to behold. For many days I did not see these things, remaining on the boat as Amerigo had asked me, so that there was time for me to reflect on my new situation, and on the unfamiliar world outside, which at first caused a trembling of my senses.

"It is very hot out there in the sun, you are fortunate to be in the cool shade," Pedro said: "we will soon retire to a quiet spot, and so ensure as little disturbance as possible to our fine-feathered friends, so that their world and our's will benefit by this meeting and not be harmed. They have been told of the presence of the great Fada in this room, and they have been awed. Your deeds have been retold to them, and your feats recounted. Their chief, who they call Cacique Pereata, has a great soft spot for you and the word has been sent out that all homage is to be paid to you and to your residence in this ship and no man is to enter within shouting distance of where it touches the water's edge. It is not bad that he has shown ease of agreement with our wishes, for humanity wherever it is found, displays the same pleasing virtues and the same displeasing vices, such as inquisitiveness and thievishness."

My diet then consisted of coconut, potato, yam, and, strange to say, dog-meat which was quite tasty and, apart from pig, was the only meat to be had. I did not like this new food at first, but as there was nothing else available, I ate it all with relish and at the heel of the hunt, I would have eaten anything.

I made other alterations in my way of life. In return for my woollen garments, I put on newly made vests of light pig's skin. A kilt of a foreign material called cotton (it is now an everyday fashion), was my trousers. But my favourite head-hat I kept, and added to it in the number of sparkling feathers which were its crown. My old friend brought these to me and they were of an astonishing variety. I remember one ... (here there was a pause and with great surprise we heard Fada addressing Pedro in person) ... do you remember it Pedro... it was very long and wide and was of the brightest blue, yellow and red in colour. It was my favourite.

"I remember it." said Pedro, "it did you credit."

I suppose these were peace-offerings, these gifts of feathers by Pedro, who realised that there was nothing to be gained from carrying on unfriendliness with Fada.

"What is Amerigo doing?", I asked courteously of him.

"He draws the mountains and the rivers, he goes into the wilderness and he puts the images of all that he sees on parchment. He is gone from morning to night on these projects."

"It is my wish to speak with Amerigo soon. Great are the plans I have and expectant my hopes in this new land."

"When we move on you will rejoice, Fada, for then you will be nearer to that final home where rest and liberty will have no limits to them. A lovely vale of palms and fruit and birds untasted before for their deliciousness will be your paradise and want will be a foreigner to you. I am a philosopher and it is true when I say that a lack of want is the best thing of all."

Those were the words of Pedro at that time.

"To lie around doing nothing is to be happy and to be happy is to be happy. You have not known the content you will know when you arrive at your final destination, Fada."

There was an interlude of a short debate between the two of them here, that we listened to with great interest.

"Pedro, you could talk a load of nonsense. Since when were you such a happy and easy-going fellow that you were satisfied to sit around and be content with what you have and be happy not to have what you haven't? Since when has a lack of want been a sure cure for ill-content? Up here there is nothing we can possess and less that we can want, for our bodies are without bone or flesh and we have no needs. The rays of life and all that is light go through us as sunlight through water in a pond, and we move around constantly like yachts on the sea, and where is our lack of discontent? You are a poor philosopher."

"And that I will say definitively, is the best kind of philosopher," Pedro answered.

It appeared to us that Pedro was treating the matter as a bit of a joke for he was speaking in a light and jolly voice and you would not believe that he intended much weight to be attached to his words.

"I suppose Pedro was assuring me of the benevolence of the world and trying to give me some cheerful encouragement. At that time he was very self-assured and he spoke with confidence. Now, I must say, the passage of centuries and having seen the events of history up to the present, has changed him quite a lot. He no more has the expectancy of seeing all he believes come true. He is a sadder and a wiser man."

After that, nobody came to me in my lonely cabin and messages to the world I sent out by loud cries over the water, through the bars of my window. No answers came back. The food I ate came from the hands of an unseen stranger who spoke no word to me nor my grasp would take in fellowship.

Then, a shock, stronger than pain, came to me when I saw in the glow of early morning, when man should be treading warily for the sake of the still-departing spirits, and the peace of night is still resting in trees and rocks: I saw with trepidation the angry sight of Pedro running behind the priest who was saying his prayers in a holy walk on the shore, and driving a sharp spear through his back, so that the man died in great agony.

★   ★   ★

A promise from a philosopher is worth more than the largest pearl in the sea, in that it is rarer; the fulfillment of a promise from a philosopher is worth less than the tiniest grain of sand on the shore, in that it is smaller.

It was a sudden fit of madness that caused him to so treacherously kill the priest, he said.

"My promise to you I had forgotten, for it is as easy to forget a promise as a curse, and it seemed the right thing to do at the time."

My rage then exceeded even his own treachery. Soon after, I saw the bold Spaniard in the midst of a multitude of scamps in rags running from the shore towards my prison-boat. It came to my mind that they had it as their purpose to kill me; and that it was Pedro himself who encouraged them in this enterprise. I think I was more surprised than a man could possibly be should he have lived a dozen lives. They were whooping and waving their arms in a pretence of bravery and weapons of all sorts were in their hands. I could see the bravest member of this army, Pedro, at the very back, crouching and hiding and encouraging them at one and the same time.

"It was not me," said Pedro, "it was somebody else who put the mob up to it. You do not find a philosopher in a mob."

Has the day come when one can disbelieve the sight of one's own eyes? Is it the case that a cat lays eggs?

The courage of those men was never seen in its likes before and it has never been seen in its likes again. For I broke the ship asunder in a rage so terrible that the sea itself trembled, and my rage was increased by the new sorrow that the boat of the worthy Amerigo Vespucci would never be able to set out on the sea again. At the moment of my appearance in the water, a roar went up from the crowd and, turning their backs to me, they fled in ignoble retreat.

It is surprising to me now that I did not chase after them, and catch my chief would-be destroyer in particular. Instead, I was to astound even myself by the loudness of the cry that came from my throat and the shouts that escaped from my lips. I vanished into the darkness of the green trees and for a long time there was nothing I was able to see, hear, taste, or remember.

An old man in the corner was making a nuisance of himself, asking questions, interrupting Fada in the course of his revelations. I was very angry with him.

"You have spent all this time listening to Fada with a face on you as long as a mile. Anyone would think you were being held in prison. Who are you to be asking questions?"

I heard him croak in reply.

"You demean every prison in the world when you compare this place to them, just as you debase the truth every time you open your mouth. What right do you have, may I ask, to rake up the dead? I was simply enquiring how much longer do we have to listen to this. At the rate he's going, we will be here till next week."

It was a typically unhelpful comment, of the kind I was used to. It displayed a woeful lack of gratitude for my efforts and a scant respect for my hard-won skill.

"It was difficult enough to get the man to talk to us in the first place. And you interrupt so that you can insult? I am not going to tolerate this. When the earth shook, and the sea was in storm and the sky was falling in on us, will be like Heaven compared to what's going to happen now. I will make you regret your insolence, you fools. The collapsing of a few walls and the ground shaking is nothing to what's about to happen. Imbeciles. If we are all alive when Fada returns, it will be a miracle. I warned you not to arouse my anger, but you did not heed."

★   ★   ★

"I am Fada. Does my story not interest you?"

"It is all right, Fada, I am still here," I said reassuringly, for he must have been calling for a long time; "you can carry on now just as you were and tell us about what happened to you in your long and eventful life."

"The woods became my home and the vines my friends. I saw there, wild animals, fleas, snails and slugs as large as the moon, bat-insects who came to devour me; long slimy

147

creatures who, with the heads of birds and the bodies of giant worms, came to frighten me and threaten me with their glinting eyes.

More incredible than the most incredible noises that ever were to come to my ears before or since, were the screeches, moans, laughter and cries of the places I passed through.

"I will say a prayer, that I may be taken out of this place," I said to myself.

I built a temple that rose above the trees, of sticks and mud and stone.

The time that passed in the making of it saw also: new moons, the numbers of whose passage were cut in a width of trees; whose extent at home would be for the sufficience of a wood to contain: a brace of wild wolves, a number of foxes equal to the number that may be counted on both hands together, a flock of birds: the cutting of deep cuts on my body and face to heal the pains of the insects; the letting loose of bird flocks as a sacrifice and as messengers of Fada.

At the end, I prepared to make my prayer to the old god we had before Patrick came. The bushes I burned in a great smoke and fire scorched the earth.

"No one is mightier than you. Not the mountains nor the ocean can go against you. Your help is pleaded for by all and your terror is famous throughout the earth. Look at this weakling below and smite him from your sight. Let him not breathe one more breath, for he is an offence to you. Destroy his temple, that is worse than a mudcabin, abandoned even by the vermin. Mock his ways, for there is laughter in the trees, the leaves weep and the flowers redden in shame. Dirt is his food and poison his drink. Finish him, for as sure as the sun sets, he will plot as the night to destroy you and all that hold sway over him."

I heard a voice reply, loud and plain.

"What can destroy you? The night is not dark to you and the heat of the jungle is cool. Strange beasts cannot harm you and the poisons are a sweetness. I put you from my mind, for you have been nothing but trouble to me. Your temple I would not use to heap manure in. You have been a nuisance to me all of your life, and a cause of distress to many innocent folk. You have destroyed the boat of my friend, Amerigo Vespucci so that now he walks sad on the sea-shore, unable to return to his home with his price-less maps. Go and throw yourself off the nearest cliff, for then some peace will come to the world."

I trembled to think of the pain and agony of a broken neck which would surely be the end result of throwing myself from a great height. And what would be my future after that? God himself was angry with me, for did I not hear his condemnation loud and plain? He would not have me into his Paradise. That much was certain.

Why did I fear now; when whole armies once threatened me, and knives were pushed in my back, but I did not worry one bit? I gambled with sharp daggers and trod lightly along steep crevices, and fear was unknown to me. Why was there such gloom in me, as I set out to find the said spot for my self-execution? Why was there a thumping like hammer-blows as I searched through that green world?

But there was no height from which Fada could throw himself. I could not find even one small cliff. The tree branches basked in the sun and the floor of the forest glittered with the sparkle of many bright things. The food of the herbs filled my stomach and the world filled my heart with a glow of fire. I hummed as I lay on the ground and listened to the talk of the forest, to the whistling and breathing from above and around. I scraped the earth for succulent roots and broke the nut-fruits from the trees.

I was in a dream, of the sort that frequently came to me in those days. I awoke to find I was sitting at the foot of a tree and I could not remember how I came to be there. In that place of much heat, I was astounded to feel great cold and my teeth were chattering. Between the trees, I saw a terrible sight appear in the sky. A horde of black demons came towards me in a wobbling flight. They vanished and there was joy in my heart at that. I blinked and opened my eyes wide. A cry escaped my lips, for the monster bats were sweeping through the sky at a rapid speed. I heard their howling and the flapping of their wings overhead. I clenched the tree and shouts and curses and spits and venom I hurled at them.

Such was my despair that I gave up hope of life. Dark was the sky with their wings and no light was I able to see at all. My heart was leaping like a wild animal inside me and my body shook as does a thin plant in the wind. A sound like that of a hundred screams came from the back of my throat, and I heard it go out into the Jungle. I closed my eyes, being afraid to open them.

When I had a glimpse through my hands at the sky above, I saw that they were gone. There was a stench in their place, like that of a rat-infested barn. I did not move or make any noise and night fell.

As the dawn of a new sun shed its light on the forest like silver thrown to poor men, I saw a lady of great beauty standing a distance away from me. It was my desire to approach her, but so great was my difficulty in arising to my feet that it was necessary for me to crawl, like those feetless creatures, and to approach her as fitfully as though I was no longer a man. Before I had reached within a close distance of her, exhaustion caused me to sink to the ground; so that my face was in the dirt and my mouth was filled with plants and moss. I wished to sleep and rest, but I was dragged along by the arms of a powerful spirit and with astonishment, I saw her as close to me as was the ground beneath. I was unable to speak. When I heard her voice, it was of a sweeter sound than any music. Her words I did not understand, but they brought peace to me. They had no beginning or end, flowing as do feathers and leaves on the water-surface.

When at last I could relieve the wonder in me, nothing was I able to understand of my own speech. I tried to praise her sufficiently, using the best and grandest words that would come from my lips. She laughed and looked with mirthful eyes at me. I was as helpless as an infant in its mother's arms; I was a Foundling before her.

For many days afterwards, I reflected on these visitations, considering if either might come back again. Though great was the fear, it was equalled by the happiness of the memory of the lady. Never before has a human of woman-flesh caused such desire in me. There was sorrow too, in that she had not willed to stay and had gone out of my sight at my approach to her.

So it was that Fada concerned himself no more with the finding of a cliff-jump, but walked at peace with himself, reflecting with his dreams and talking to all that was about him. His talk was that of the wild, its words were nature's language, meaningful not to humans but to simple creatures, such as the animals of the trees, who were always aware of Fada's presence, watching him from afar and knowing the times of his sadness and gladness; his hours of peace and of anger too.

Under the shadow of a great moon, when the singers of the night were joined in a chorus that reached up to the heavenly bodies, and Fada's dream was filling his whole mind in a hymn of fulfilment, a silver river appeared that was as wide as the sea, and his eyes were opened in surprise and the singing of the night ceased. It was there at that place that he settled to rest and ceased his travelling. From the back of a dead animal he cut the single garment he wore. His hair was long like the beards of the trees. In his arm was a vine-rope, for gully-crossings and the binding of things. A tree-trunk was his shelter and a hole there was for the storing of his nuts.

Fada was at the end of the world, where there was no dispute between men. No jealous foe or thieving friend came to annoy him. He gathered in many things, feathers in a multitude, flowers of the rainbow, stones of odd shapes. To sink in the water was a pleasure, and he lay back on his hands, looking at the sky and the trees above and calling at the birds as they flew about.

In the heat of the noon-sun, when peaceful sleep had closed the eye-lids of the tired wanderer, and the birds washed themselves in the flashing water, there came into the glade many brown men, with scowls on their faces and spears in their hands. Fada was woken by the pushing of a sharp stick in his belly.

"So it is the brown men. You are all very small. Why have you come into the home of Fada and disturbed his peace?"

They pulled me with much determination, in order that I might accompany them back into the forest, but I did not move and grievous was their disappointment. Yells and tears did they give and they broke their implements against the trunks of trees and on the ground in anger. Many hours later they returned, as the sun was resting in the lower branches and preparing its tired face for sleep. Their numbers had increased, so that now there was a vast multitude, and there came also many chiefs, whose headdresses had hosts of feathers. With much talk and persuasion, they invited me to return with them to their city, which would make a big noise at my entrance. Fada went, glad at last for the company of men.

There was wonderment in my eyes when I saw the town of their settlement, for I believed I had come again to my own home in far-away Ireland, there being no difference between the baile of Fada and the village of these wild ones. It was a home-coming for me as I went in through the gates, being welcomed on all sides, at front and behind. My sight was immediately disposed to see the cut-off heads of men strung from poles around me. With smiles and head-gestures and strange words they told me they had taken the heads of their enemies whom they called "Arawak" and they kept the women of these foes for their own use. The men of the Arawaks were weak and cowardly, who were content to make gardens and spend their days at land-labour, but their women-kind were handsome and loving.

"I have come from the land of the shamrock. I will tell you my story until the stars have gone out and the sun's forehead comes up on the roofs and on the footways and the night no longer listens to itself and all the world hears again the hum of its own life and when my story may sleep in the minds of men. I dream of the land from which I come, a land of grass as rich as wine, of rain as gentle as the caress of the angel of sleep, feasts that give food and drink to men and wind that washes away the cares and sins of all; I long for the sight of cows munching lazily in the mist; these I once possessed in over-large numbers, but they were taken from me. My sight is pained from the absence of a cow or beast, which I have not seen in the New World. The sound of cow-noise is absent to me, and the taste of cow-milk forgotten."

They sat down by the fireside. The tobacco they smoked and offered to me, I refused.

"There was one who lived within a bird-call of Fada, whose daughter was betrothed to him, the likes of whose treachery has been unknown in its immensity to man before, and whom Fada caused to be removed from the company of the living, who stole the cattle of Fada and put there in their place, anger and new wisdom. But so great was the sorrow, and so small the forgiveness of a man so wretchedly wronged, that a curse fell on him, and he was a stranger for evermore in foreign parts. In some lands he was famous and he was despised in others. As often as unruly men were shouting his praises, they called for him to be run out. There is no peace in the cities of men, and hunger and solitude are preferable to feasting and laughter."

"There is a sadness in the Caribe people at the sight of Fada, for though your words are not understandable to them, the telling of your story is a cause of much distress and pain. They are a vicious people and are feared even by me their own chief, who would never turn his back to the closest of his brother Caribes; pain is pleasure to them and happiness is not in their understanding, and yet see: I do not believe what I see: they are weeping for Fada. You are a wonder to appear before us and I do not know what will be the result of this appearance. Can you of the great white hair that covers your face and is as long as the trees, who are a man but of a kind never seen before, be a cause of new wisdom among my people? Then you will be a greater curse to me than is all the goodness of the land, for wisdom is happiness, which I do not wish for my restless people. Tell them of your mighty killings and of how you plundered the weak and the childish."

"You bite me hard so that your teeth tell me of your anger. There are many things to relate of: the robbing of the King of France and the World of his army, the shaking of the chief city of France, the subduing of the man of Rome. These deeds gave joy and glory to Fada. He came with Pedro and Amerigo to the New World, and there he saw the treachery of one, and he broke the boat of Amerigo, so that the heart of Fada was wrenched. No friends now he has and he listens to no one but speaks only to himself. Weakened is his strength so that his proud jump he no longer performs, and men take him and command him to speak as they please.''

''I will cut the tongue from your mouth, you, man-monkey with the skin of death, whose eyes are soul-less blue water; anger steals my patience like a thief and dark clouds of fury descend over me. You have brought much disturbance to my people. They weep at the sorrow in your speech and in your face. They have no hate or rapacity and are full of pity and tenderness. Remove yourself from my city, for I will not poison my pots with your wicked flesh. Live with the mad ones and those diseased and bent of the body in the bitter exile of the forest. My people will forget the trickery of your talk and peace will return. Woe to the day I brought you here and a death worse than that of a common Arawak I deserve. I will punish myself later when you are gone.''

So it was that I returned to the forest and sought out again my quiet place on the river-bank. But peace had gone and a new disquiet was in me. So great was the disturbance in Fada, that he could not stay still, but he constantly walked about in an agitation. No clothes now did he wear, so that he was naked as the trees are to the wind. His loins burned, so that his desire was overwhelming and all-powerful. The madness in him increased as he sought around him release from the new curse that had come down. He dreamt of Pegeen, whose value to him now was higher than the value to be placed on all the cows in Ireland. Also of Andree, who had followed him in Paris, and the young maid he put to death. He heard them calling him in the loud winds and they whispered to him in the gentle breeze. In the daylight also, he saw them, as they washed in the flowing waters, and lay in the cool shade of the palm trees. To call to them was to bring forth a silence quieter than is the tomb; to approach them was to find scorpions and thorns.

The exile of the moon was not worse than the exile of Fada. He envied the trees which grew in company with one another; the flowers which the bees visited; he envied the little animals and birds that came and went not as one, but in multitudes. While Fada was alone, all nature was together and bitter was the pain that the knowledge of this made in him. He listened as the river water flowed freely and contentedly in its talk with the land. He heard the sigh of the trees in their embrace of the wind. The land beckoned to all its neighbours; from afar came the wind and the rain, the moon and the sun. In all of this Fada was not a part, for who was to hearken to his call and receive his embrace? When tiredness made weary his bones and he lay in the forest, like an unwanted guest at a great king's feast, his sleep would be haunted by dreams and strange desires, which were new and incomprehensible to him. For a long time it was this way with Fada. It became so that he knew neither peace of mind nor the pain of the lack or it; not the comfort of hope nor the resignation of despair. His body no longer was a pride to him, but he kept it as a man might keep an unwanted dog. His own words and his own prayers he did not hear. Sometimes a bird whistle or a twig break caused him to stop at their sound, in a mystery and incomprehension of mind.

And now my story is nearly at an end, for the last days of Fada were approaching. But they did not find a sad Fada when they came, but a happy one, whose happinesses could be counted above the stars, being beyond measure. The husbandless women of the Arawak took him,: and were glad of him, and idolised him. As numerous as the blossoms of the flowers every day of the year were his descendants, who came to inhabit every part of the forest and the river, and went out to dwell in the plains and on the coast of the sea. Great blessings were showered on Fada, so that no more was he alone at night or at any hour of the day. No more either did be hear the tree wind or see the sun rise, for nothing lived apart from Fada and he was the voice of the forest.

# Chapter Ten

"Well there is no doubt that Pada is still up to his best when it comes to talk. I suppose it is the drink that has loosened his tongue, for I haven't heard so much out of him in ages. Pedro, for it is I who speak, lost the friendship of Fada for the killing of an untrustworthy priest. I said to him afterwards if everyone has to die sometime, what does it matter if death should come to him earlier, or by what means? Is it not so that by being born, everyman is condemned to die and so it is wrong to accuse a person of being a murderer when he accomplishes for nature what she has in mind in any case? Fada accepted my argument and he forgave me and we are still the best of friends, ever since we came together up here."

"Let me ask you a question, Pedro, for I am sure you really are a philosopher, and that that which you have debated on and stated is really true. Has it been as you thought it would be, life after death?" "The only extant manuscript of mine, which was read out to you, stated certain objective beliefs concerning death which I held at the time. It would be wrong for me to hold still to these conclusions, considering the facts as they presently stand. However, let me tell you that in one very important respect I was correct. The body does not live on after death. We are all-spirit up here.''

"This is very interesting, Pedro. I must say it is a pleasure to be talking to you and to be listening to you, about whom we have been hearing so much. Let me ask you one thing. Where is the manuscript of your's that you say is still around? Would it be very valuable, for instance? Do you think that if what is in it is incorrect, or is completely out-of-date, that this would have a very big effect on its value?''

"I see that you are in a danger of becoming a bit of a philosopher yourself. Let us leave these matters alone, for I have no doubt there are many questions on the tip of your tongue, not a small number of which I would not be in a position to answer right now. Let me ask you a question. Do you believe what Fada is saying?''

I had to think about what I was going to say now, as Heaven knows, the whole thing was moving along at a rapid pace and showing signs at the same time of even becoming more involved. There was this Pedro with whom I felt no kinship at all, maybe because of his supposed Spanish origin, although I can't imagine that they would have him in Spain, even by his own account. I always believe in humouring story-tellers and in giving them the run of the shop, as it were, as long as we can all stick to the main business in hand. We were there to hear Fada's tale, and we were more than willing to listen to Pedro, as long as he enlightened us further on the times and events of the Irishman's life, with which he had obviously much to do. But the last thing we wanted now was, with the dawn coming up on the east, to lose touch with Fada and hear no more from him. I for one, was interested in his story and in hearing it all from start to finish.

"Let him carry on and we will judge the truth of what he has said at the end," I stated firmly, considering it an adequate reply.

"Does your audience believe what he says?", asked Pedro, not to be put off, I suppose.

"Those of them who remain do believe," I assured him angrily, "I have dealt with the others."

I heard a long laugh from Pedro at this and then he asked in a half serious and half jocund tone of voice:

"Can you make sure that enough are here at the end?"

"I will try, Pedro," I rather ironically assured him:

"I suppose Fada is gone off drinking. How, may I ask, if it is not too rude a question, is it possible for a man to drink who has no body? There are bound to be the doubters still left with us, who will be worrying themselves to death I am sure, by the profundity of this question. Can you put their troubled thoughts at ease and give their poor souls some peace at last?"

"I am always willing to listen to a man's question. Yes, he has gone for a drink again, as the talking has put a strain on him as it would on anybody, who has given a discourse of such length. However, it is not possible to drink up here, for even if we had gullets and bellies and so forth, there would be no means whatsoever of obtaining the liquids. As I told you before, Fada has to pretend about many things. When I say that he has gone for a drink, what is meant is that he is imagining that he is alive again and sitting in a snug inn, enjoying himself. He does that a lot of the time."

"Another question for you, Pedro. Are you a Spaniard?"

"I am from Spain, yes."

160

"As a matter of interest, is Amerigo Vespucci there with you?"

"They will have to think up a new name for me soon, as I seem to be the man who answers all questions and provides all the solutions to life. Anyway, it is not your fault and I always try to help out. I have not seen sight or heard sound of him. Fada has not either. Are you satisfied?"

"Thanks. What kind of a man was he? He must have had great virtues and been an inspiration to live and work with. I suppose you saw his good points and his bad points."

"Amerigo Vespucci has become very famous in history. I was never able to discover what his nationality was. He was, most of the time, a jealous man, who was wont to resent other people their good fortune, and he was apt to have a boundless hatred for any person who bettered him in anything. That applied not only to his arch-rival, Columbus, but to everyone. I have seen him in a fury with ordinary, simple sailors who had made the mistake of being more cheerful then he was in the morning, or of pointing out to his notice routine matters concerning the ship or voyage that had escaped his own attention. I am afraid he was not a perfect man. He was not a saintly man. He is up there in the gallery of heroes now, a gallery which has its fair share of rascals. But he was a very clever man, and I was not bored with him. He was good company."

"How did he get on in the New World?"

There was a very long silence from Pedro following this question. I thought that maybe he didn't want to tell us anything about it, or on the other hand, that he was taking his time thinking up what to say.

"Amerigo made the first map of the continent we had discovered. He put it on a sheet of white parchment and across it he wrote his name, Amerigo, as evidence of its authorship. This was something he was to regret later. Then, when a boat called in, he had this map sent back to his friend, Waldseemuller of Berlin, a person of a very similar frame of mind to Amerigo. He sent a note also with it, explaining it was his intention to name the place 'Fada'. He asked that no other name should be applied to it. The idiot Waldseemuller wrote 'Amerigo's map' on it and sent it to the printers, so America it's called now. When Fada so suddenly went into the bushes and did not come out again, a great sorrow overcame Amerigo so that he wept without ceasing. He made many searches in the interior and a gloom worse than that of a thousand nights stuck in Madrid was with him wherever he went. For many years he awaited the return of Fada. In the end he gave up and went home, broken in spirit, to Europe."

"What was life like in the New World?", I asked Pedro. When his voice returned, it was heavy with emotion.

"It could have been fine. It was Amerigo's fault that things did not turn out as they should have. That cretin brought his woman with him on the ship and later he concealed her in his hut, so that we were not supposed to be aware of her presence. When this gross dishonesty, this irresponsible act, was discovered, there was a mutiny among the men. A proclamation was issued by them, in which demands were made of Amerigo: that he give to them the head of his woman on a platter; or else that she be released to them, to be shared by one and all. It was demanded also that I, Pedro, be made to leave the camp.... ."

There was another pause in Pedro's talk. I suppose he was living again through what were probably tragic, emotional experiences.

"There was no peace after that. It was necessary for Amerigo and I to arm ourselves and to be ever-watchful for our lives from that time on. There was no hope anymore that we could establish a peace-loving community of hard-working and self-sacrificing people, intent only on living in peace and brotherhood with their brown neighbours. For all of this, Amerigo was to blame. That was the one thing about Amerigo – he did not understand human nature. Here comes Fada."

"Pedro. Before you go. Tell us what happened to you."

"It is none of your business."

"I am Fada. It is no use asking Pedro such questions. He was never one for talking about himself. The end of Pedro is something I have not been able to find any information about. I know that he must have lived a long time afterwards, for he had my gold to help him do it. One day, when I was very old and so hard and solid was the sleep in my eyes that I had difficulty in opening them, I heard a commotion around me and felt myself being lifted and carried in the arms of many men. We came into a camp of burning fires, where multitudes of people had gathered. It was the day, and the noon sun was in my eyes and circles of light and colour were dancing everywhere. There was a beating of loud drums and the stamping of many feet. They were preparing to eat Fada, who lay exposed and patient before them. It was then, when I became fully awake, that I considered on many things and awaited, with no fear, the end. My mother was dead and she had always been unknown to me; my heart went out to my grand-aunt Aine, who would be very old and who had looked after me as her own son. I was sorrowful now that I could not send word to her. For long minutes I thought on her virtues and praised her for the goodness she had shown to me.

When the moment of my killing came, I asked if I might do one thing before my life was taken from me. I was granted this last wish. I took my bag of gold from its most secret of hiding-places, so that I might look on it. I had great difficulty in untying the string, so tight was it and so cumbersome were my fingers. When I looked inside, I found that the gold was gone. It had been stolen. I immediately surmised that the thief was Pedro. Instead of a huge anger, there was only sorrow in my heart at the deed and a great pity for the philosopher. Almost as soon as the surprise of this was making itself known to me, there was another surprise in that I found in the bag a white pigeon-breasted bird that I had never before seen in my life. I still do not know where it came from. It was a blessing to me for I knew at once what I must do with it. From my clothes I took a ring on which was my name, and I put this on the leg of the bird. When it was done, I sent it on its long journey to Ireland and prayed that one day it would be received by my aunt.

It was a happy and contented Fada who submitted to the multitude then. There is not much that I remember of the last moments, but one thought is still very clear in my mind. It was a regret that in all my travels and in all the places I visited, I never performed the ultimate version of the Lame. This was something that had held them spell-bound at fairs and feiseanna in Ireland long ago; it was to carry two jugs of foaming beer in my hands and drink them while suspended from a great height. It was a sight and a half."

★   ★   ★

"It goes without saying that Pedro did not steal the gold; for one reason alone if for no other; I did not know where it was to be found. Many times then and since, I have doubted the existence of such a thing at all, for I have never known a man to talk so much about something, for whose presence there was such little evidence. Many times

I have said to him: if it is gone, why don't you tell me where it was you kept it hidden? Why not tell me and the people down there right now the marvellous hiding spot you were able to think up?"

"All right boys, pack it up. We have to go. It's morning."

I could not believe that the time had gone so fast and it was the best session that I had ever arranged. It was the most interesting by far. I was proud of Fada.

"It is not the end yet. Fada and I need your help in a matter of major importance. We want your advice. We are willing, believe it or not, to place our destiny in your hands."

Pedro had spoken these words.

"Can you tell me what this is all about?," I asked.

"Fada is fed up being here. He no longer listens to me when I advise patience and waiting. He wants to go out the door. I have come to agree with him. I no longer wish to hang around this place. I am going to go against my own advice."

"Well there is nobody stopping you, is there?"

"The problem is which door should we go out? There is the front door and the back door here and we don't know where either one leads."

"And what can we do in the matter?"

"It is my belief that one of these doors opens to a world of eternal peace and rest, but that the second one leads into that other place, you know? I think any sympathetic person will be able to see our predicament. Neither I nor Fada wish to take on the responsibility of choosing either door."

"Is there no way you can tell which is the right door? I always figure that a front one is better than a back one."

"They are both alike. There is no difference between them. That is the problem. If the front door were bigger and finer than the back, I would be out through it in a flash.''

"Perhaps the two of them lead into the good world. How do you know that something different lies behind each?''

"You certainly have a critical mind. We long ago considered that point. And in the end, we came up with this question. If the two of them lead into the same place, why was one door not good enough? Put that in your pipe and smoke it.''

"O.K. Point taken. What is it you want us to do?''

"You can decide for us.''

If you ask me, I don't see why they couldn't have chosen a door for themselves long ago. And in the first place, it is a mystery to me how they could have got into this predicament.

"It is a heavy responsibility all right. I will ask the opinion of the audience.''

"That is what we want. Whatever decision is taken, it will be out of our hands. Should it be the wrong decision, we need not blame ourselves. Should it be the right one, well then of course there is no problem and we will be eternally grateful to you.''

I turned to address myself to the sitters.

"Let us have a show of hands and resolve a matter of the utmost importance. I need not remind you that whatever you decide, it will have eternal implications. It is nothing more or less than that. Issues of this kind properly belong in the hands of the gods, but since it has come to us, let us not shirk a grave duty. Which shall it be then, the front door or the back door?''

I was very amused when I saw that they were not making any effort to help out. And such is the nature of man, that when he is faced with a matter of destiny, he will turn his tiny head and try to ignore Fate staring him in the face. He will be too preoccupied with his own petty or imaginary injuries and his indestructible selfishness. He will turn his face on what is great, and lose himself in the dust and the sand.

Our friends listening there were no different.

"All right then. Let us look at it this way. The sooner we decide on something, the sooner we can be finished here. You need not take the issue seriously."

"We don't want to get involved. We want nothing to do with this!", said the old critter in the corner.

"If I had a bucket of sand here, I would give it to you so that you could bury your head in it. I have a plan. I am going to ask you to vote on whether we should leave here. I am going to say two words: front and back. If you put up your hands, I will inform Pedro of how many go up each time. As far as yourselves are concerned, you can take it that you are simply voting to have these proceedings finished with and to be away. And nothing else. You can consider yourselves entirely innocent of the fate of Pedro and Fada."

They agreed to put up their hands, but only to show that they wanted the session to end.

"Now the problem is, which do I say first?"

Naturally there was nobody to help me out here either.

"It will have to be one or the other. I guess I will toss a coin to decide."

I threw up a coin and caught it as it came down.

"Front for front and back for back. The back door it is."

They all put up their hands.

"That leaves us with the front door."

There were no hands.

I passed on the word to Pedro. There was the sound of loud slamming and terror appeared on the faces of everyone present. There was a sudden rush from the room and much shouting and pushing. I was left alone there. I stood up and went to let in the light. I got a broom and began sweeping the floor for it was very dusty and I also lit a cigarette. I puffed it with a smile of satisfaction and I waited for Pedro and Fada himself to come in the door.